Becoming English

CW00738897

EVA TUCKER was born in Be
child. Her early novels *Contact* ___ _ __ _____ ___ ___ _____
by Calder & Boyars in the 1960s. Her stories have appeared
in *London Magazine* and elsewhere, as well as being broadcast
by the BBC; her acclaimed recent novel, *Berlin Mosaic*, was
published by Starhaven in 2005. Quaker by convincement, she
ran the Hampstead Interfaith Group for many years and has
served on the Writers in Prison Committee of English PEN.
She lives in London.

The cover of this book incorporates an image from artist
Judith Tucker's collection *Tense*, entitled 'Springboard (i)'.

To Pat from Eva   May 2009

BECOMING ENGLISH

by

Eva Tucker

© 2009 Eva Tucker
ISBN 0-936315-28-8

STARHAVEN, 42 Frognal, London NW3 6AG
in U.S., c/o Box 2573, La Jolla, CA 92038
books@starhaven.org.uk
www.starhaven.org.uk

Typeset in Dante by John Mallinson
Printed by CPI, 38 Ballard's Lane, London N3 2BJ

for my daughters

Judith, Catherine & Sarah

Outside, a fierce February wind whistles through the trees. Inside, a little girl sees her pale face reflected in the mirror of the station waiting-room.

'Is this me?' Laura asks herself.

A woman is sitting beside her, shivering. Ruth is her mother, but Laura cannot make her feel quite real now that they are in Somerset and not Berlin. She will *not* cry; she is nearly ten years old. If only her granny and grandpa and her father were there, too! Her grandpa said he was much too old to change countries; he was German first, Jewish second, no one would touch him. And, of course, her granny would not come away without him. Her father, who is not Jewish, will not abandon the country he loves. He has arranged for Laura and Ruth, from whom he is divorced, to stay with his English Quaker friend Miss Tate.

Here she is, tall and thin and white-haired, coming to pick them up. She smiles towards them.

'Ruth, Laura, meine Lieben!' She speaks good German.

It is dusk by the time they drive up a cinder path through a white five-barred gate.

'Welcome to Meadow House!'

A light comes on above the front door. Two tall figures emerge, one with a brown knitted hood hiding her face, the other with silvery hair shining like a crown under the light. They go inside, where a little dog with silky blond hair is wagging its tail.

'His name is Barney,' the woman in the brown hood says.

Laura pats him and he licks her hand. *Feels lovely,* she thinks.

'These are my friends Miss Harvill and Miss Croft; we all live in Meadow House,' Miss Tate says. Laura's mother shakes hands with them; Laura bobs a curtsy. The three old ladies smile. Has she done something funny?

A little later, still clutching the raffia chimney sweep her father gave her for good luck just before the train pulled out of the Anhalter Bahnhof, she goes to sleep next to her mother in the servants' bedroom. When she wakes up, she is not quite sure where she is. Of course, she is in England!

Every morning she has an English lesson with Miss Tate. They read a book about a girl called Rhoda who goes to boarding school, is a good sport and plays lacrosse, which she calls 'lax'. Laura has no idea what sort of game that is.

'As soon as your English is good enough, you'll go to a school rather like that,' Miss Tate tells her.

'And play lacrosse?'

'I think they play netball and hockey at Mentmore House, where you'll be going.'

At least Laura has heard of those games. In Berlin they played handball; she was not much good at it.

Miss Croft and Miss Harvill speak English to Laura all the time. When she does not quite understand, Miss Tate translates. There is a list of new words for Laura to remember every day. Usually she remembers them quite well, except one or two, like *promise* and *suppose.* For some reason she finds those difficult.

'Promise to remember *promise,*' Miss Tate says.

The old ladies give her English children's books to look at.

She gets to know Moly and Ratty in *The Wind in the Willows* and the Philosopher in the *Crock of Gold*. She already knows *Alice in Wonderland* and *Little Lord Fauntleroy*: her father gave her those in German.

One afternoon two real English girls come to tea. They are called Penelope and Angela and talk very fast, saying things like *Don't be pernickety* and *It's all higgledy piggledy*. Laura has never heard the name Penelope, but Angela is familiar, except that at home it is pronounced *Anghela* with a hard g. She is getting used to sounding her g's soft like j's. Not always, though. English pronunciation is hard to get right all the time. With a start she realises she has just thought *at home* meaning Berlin, meaning her granny and grandpa, her father. But that is not *at home* any longer. Where is that now? She falls silent; Penelope and Angela go on talking to each other.

Laura's mother Ruth has hardly stopped crying since they arrived. She cries most when there are letters from Berlin but also because she does not like being the old ladies' housemaid.

'I'm not a housemaid. I'm a physiotherapist!' she sobs.

Ruth got herself trained in Berlin and talked enthusiastically about how she would help people recovering from injuries. There was such a glow about her then! Laura knows her mother hates housework, but it was the only condition on which she was allowed into England.

Miss Harvill shows Ruth how to lay a fire in the grate with twists of newspaper and twigs under the rectangles of peat.

'One match should be enough!' Miss Harvill says, but Ruth needs at least half a dozen matches to get the fire going – in Berlin there was central heating. Quite soon, Ruth asks permission to go to London: she wants to find work with a Jewish family. She has to ask permission because she needs the train fare. They were not allowed to bring any money out of Germany and she only gets a pound a week for the housework she hates doing. Most of that goes on cigarettes from the village shop. Sometimes Ruth gives Laura threepence to spend on those cushion-shaped peppermints called humbugs. The three old ladies look disapproving when they see Ruth light a cigarette; Laura decides she will not smoke when she grows up.

'Perhaps you will be happier with your own people,' Miss Tate says tersely. Laura knows Miss Tate means other Jewish people. She thinks: *I'm only half Jewish.* She has not thought that since she arrived in England and she does not want to think it now; she is fed up with not being quite this or that. At her Jewish school in Berlin the others would say incredulously: *your father's a goy?* She never got to know *his* parents, who live in Thüringen. In case her being half Jewish might have been embarrassing for them. Here in England she can grow whole.

Ruth hugs and kisses Laura as she leaves. 'Very, very soon I come to fetch you!' But Laura does not want to be fetched: she likes it where she is.

When Ruth has gone, Miss Tate, Miss Croft and Miss Harvill say they would like Laura to call them Aunt Ann, Aunt Edwina and Aunt Tessa. They seem to feel she might be missing her mother, but Laura is relieved. Having Ruth about was making it much harder to try and become English. How long will it take?

The honorary aunts take her to a fête at the Women's Institute. Aunt Tessa – the one with the silvery hair – wins first prize for her flower arrangement. Her cheeks, which are like chamois leather, go quite pink. Laura wishes her granny were with them. A parson in a long black cassock comes up to them.

'So this is our little refugee girl,' he says and takes her by the hand. 'Are you coming to gamble with me?'

Does he know she is half-Jewish? That she has never been in a church? At the shove-a-ha'penny stall the parson quickly loses all the ha'pence he rolls onto the oilcloth marked out in squares.

'Now we shall never mend the church roof,' he says cheerfully. When he hands her back to the honorary aunts, he pats her on the head.

'Poor mite!' he says.

Laura has no idea a mite is, but she can feel it has something to do with being a refugee. In the car on the way back home (yes, Laura has thought *home* about Meadow House) she asks, 'When will I stop being a refugee?' She does not feel like one. She feels like her grandpa's 'little rascal', like her granny's 'darling goldfinch', like her father's 'big girl' who is allowed to ask him any questions she likes. She wishes she could ask *him* how long it will take to stop being a refugee. And then she smiles to herself, thinking of the child-sized coat hanger he gave her. It has *For the good child* printed on one side (in German, of course); with indelible pencil her father printed *For the naughty child* on the other side. *So you can use it every day,* he said and kissed her on the forehead. She has brought that hanger with her. Laura notices tears are trickling down her cheeks. When they get back to Meadow House, Aunt Tessa asks if she would like to give Barney his supper.

Every morning, indoors in the workroom or, if it is fine, outside on the terrace called the sun parlour, Aunt Ann brushes the tangles and burrs out of Barney's coat. Laura helps pull the burrs out as gently as she can, but Barney always yelps. When the brushing is done, he jumps off Aunt Ann's knee, shakes himself and turns round and round. Aunt Ann hands Laura two bone-shaped biscuits.

'Make him sit!'

Laura says 'Sit' as sternly as she can.

Barney sits: she gives him the biscuits; his warm tongue lollops over her palm. *Barney likes me,* she thinks – *Barney hat mich gerne.* It doesn't matter whether she thinks it in English or German, Barney likes her anyway. She runs out into the garden with him.

Picture postcards arrive from her father, long letters from her granny asking for details of all her doings; her grandpa adds a few lines in spidery writing that Laura finds it hard to read. Aunt Ann gives her writing paper and envelopes and she switches back to thinking in German in her replies. There is a letter from Ruth calling her *My darling independent daughter* and telling her that soon, soon they will be together again. That letter makes Laura's heart sink. She is looking forward to going to a school like Rhoda's in the book which she can now read by herself. She writes to her mother saying how much she likes it in Meadow House and that she can't wait to go to school; so, when, just before the beginning of the summer term, Ruth reappears, Laura is not pleased.

'You come viz me to London now, you come vair you belong viz your muzzer!' Ruth is speaking English.

'But I'm going to boarding school!' Laura bursts into tears.

The honorary aunts ask Laura to come and visit them in Meadow House whenever she likes. She wishes and wishes she did not have to leave.

So then she is on a train to London with her mother. Ruth has found a job as house help with an Orthodox Jewish family in Stamford Hill. Laura is allowed to sleep there, but she has to be out during the day. Émigré friends from Berlin who live in Golders Green have offered to look after her. Laura travels across London by herself. 'You haf to learn to be independent,' Ruth tells her, not for the first time. Laura got to hear that quite often, even in Berlin. She has to change buses; the conductor tells her where to get off; then she asks a policeman the way. You don't have to be frightened of policemen in England; they're called Bobbies.

There is chocolate pudding for afters which the friends have made as a special treat.

'Just like your granny used to make,' they say; but it is not in the least as delicious as her granny's.

'At Meadow House we had spotted dick or treacle tart or apple crumble for pudding; the apples were from the garden,' she informs the family. When she sees them look rather crestfallen, she wishes she had not mentioned it.

Ruth picks her up in the evenings. When they get back to Stamford Hill, there are always men washing their hands and mumbling Hebrew prayers. They smile at Laura and go on praying. She has never met people like them before. In Berlin the family only went to synagogue on High Holidays.

After two or three weeks of this to-ing and fro-ing, Ruth tells Laura she has found a family in Northolt, just outside London, who want to look after a little refugee girl. That phrase again!

'But why can't I go back to Meadow House?'

Laura misses life in Somerset. Most of all she misses Barney. The family who want to look after a little refugee girl have a dog, too, a black Scottie called Trixie. And they have a son the same age as Laura, called Arthur. His father plays cricket with them in the long narrow garden at the back of the house. Laura has never seen anyone play cricket; she learns to bowl with a soft ball when Arthur shouts *ploy* (she knows it means *play*). They go to watch a cricket match, and Laura enjoys looking at the men in their white flannels, but it goes on for a very long time and she does not quite follow the rules, though Arthur's father explains everything. Laura notices that Arthur is totally absorbed in the match, so she tries not to feel bored.

She goes to the same school as Arthur, but he does not walk with her. He has his own friends – boys, of course. She walks a little way behind them.

'She's got to take a test with MD children,' she hears Arthur tell his friends. She catches up with him.

'What's MD?' she asks.

'Loonies!' Arthur taps his forehead.

There are questions like: *a violin, a drum, a flute, a cauliflower, a piano – which does not belong to the group?* She passes the test, but she does not mention it when she writes to her father and her grandparents. She tells them about weaving a tea cosy with a thing called a *heddle*, about country dancing, about singing *If all the world were paper, and all the sea were ink.*

Occasionally, Laura is first back in the house after school. Only Trixie is there. She takes the dog into the garden, where the raspberries are ripe on their canes. Arthur's mother makes delicious jam with them, which they quite often have for tea. *I'll just have a few; it won't matter,* Laura thinks. There is something so special about eating fruit you have picked yourself. She is still stuffing them into her mouth when Arthur's mother comes home.

'Arthur doesn't do that,' she says gently.

Laura wishes she had not eaten so many raspberries, but she has. She starts to cry. Arthur's mother hugs her.

'Never mind now, dear,' she says. 'Worse things 'appen at sea,' Arthur's father says when he hears what she has done. Laura is not quite sure what that means, but she can tell he is not angry with her.

At the beginning of the summer holidays, Ruth arrives one Saturday afternoon to say that now, because almost certainly there will be war, Laura is to go back to Meadow House. Laura is delighted: it feels almost as if she is going home. She will see Barney! Though she has made friends with Trixie, she knows that the Scottie likes Arthur best. By the time she leaves that kind family who have taught her the rules of cricket, her English is fluent and she thinks in German only when there is post from Berlin.

Ruth tells Laura about a pamphlet she has been given called *A Helpful Guide for Every Refugee,* published by British Jews. There are lists of things refugees must and must not do: *don't speak German too loudly in the street; don't read German in public; don't criticise government regulations; don't take part in political activities; don't dress conspicuously; remember the English attach great importance to modesty; understatement in speech rather than overstatement.*

'Ze English Jews tell us how ve have to behave. Zey sink ve give zem a bad name!' Ruth says.

The Golders Green friends who looked after Laura did speak German in the street quite loudly and, even when they spoke English, Laura thinks, it *sounded* like German. But, no, they did not dress conspicuously.

Ruth puts Laura on the train to Bridgwater at Paddington and asks the guard to keep an eye on her.

'Just arrived over 'ere?' he asks Laura.

She tells him she has already been in England for six months.

''Ave yer an' all,' he says and winks at her.

She tries to wink back but cannot quite manage it. The guard laughs, and Laura laughs with him. He helps her off the train with her case.

All three honorary aunts are on the platform to meet her.

Laura hopes they will be pleased with the way her English has come on, but she notices that they look at each other in a peculiar way when she asks if she should shut the *gite* and tells them about *ploying* cricket.

'You've turned into a proper little Cockney, haven't you?' Aunt Ann says.

Aunt Edwina pats her on the head and explains that Cockney is a particular London kind of English. They do not say that it is not good English, but Laura knows from the way they correct her that it is not. She begins to realise that there are different ways of being English.

War is declared at the beginning of September. They listen to the Prime Minister Neville Chamberlain broadcast: *I prayed that the responsibility might not fall upon me to ask this country to accept the awful arbitrament of war... We have no quarrel with the German people, except that they allow themselves to be governed by a Nazi government. As long as that government exists and pursues the methods it has so persistently followed during the last two years, there will be no peace in Europe...*

Ruth is staying in Meadow House for a few days. She has found a new housekeeping job.

'Viz educated people, also from Berlin.'

The aunts are very kind to her, call her *Ruth my dear* and look serious when the grandparents are mentioned; all German Jews who have not got away are in grave danger now.

Laura is relieved when Ruth goes back to London: it is so much easier to turn into her new English self without her mother. She sits with the honorary aunts round the peat fire sewing brass rings on the inside of the black-lined curtains so that they can be stretched tightly across the windows and fastened on to hooks that Ben the gardener has screwed in. No chink of light must be seen from the outside; there will be air

10

raids. Laura does not feel frightened; inside herself she feels safe.

'We remember the outbreak of the first world war,' Aunt Ann says.

'We hoped and prayed it would be the last!' And then she adds 'Your father will not have to fight. He was injured in the last war.'

'My father's not a Nazi!' Laura says hotly.

'Unthinkable! We tried so hard to persuade him to come out of Germany,' Aunt Ann goes on, 'but he would not, he loves his country. We understand and respect that.' Aunt Ann speaks with great affection about him.

They go on to talk about their local MP who got elected as an Independent. 'Such an astute man,' Aunt Tessa says. *Astute* – a new word for Laura to look up in the dictionary.

'I wish we had more Independents,' Aunt Edwina says, and then, looking at Laura, 'It means he doesn't have to vote with either of the main parties. Still, now there's a war on, we'll almost certainly have a coalition government.'

Coalition – another new word.

'We'll have the best brains in the country working together!'

Laura begins to feel it is her country.

§

Towards the middle of September Aunt Ann says, 'Beginning of term next week!'

Laura has got her school uniform – royal blue tunic, white blouse, royal blue jumper, royal blue bloomers for gym. *Bloomers* – what is the connection between blooms and knickers? There isn't any; it's just that English is so peculiar. She has black stockings, indoor shoes, outdoor shoes. Her navy blue coat from Berlin still fits her.

'And we'll get second hand Sunday uniform for you at school, and a blue velveteen dress for Friday evenings.'

Sunday uniform? Friday evenings? Laura says nothing, but she is puzzled. Friday evenings are Jewish; Sundays are Christian. Which are for her?

Aunt Ann and Aunt Edwina drive Laura to Mentmore House School in Weston-Super-Mare on a Sunday afternoon. Aunt Edwina has come with them because she was at school with the younger of the Misses Thomas, the sisters who are the headmistresses. Laura cannot imagine Aunt Edwina at school; her skin is so wrinkled and her mouth a bit crooked, because she has had a stroke. Only her blue eyes set deep in her face have stayed young. She and Aunt Ann, who is driving, are arguing about whether driving fast or slowly uses less petrol. Going downhill, Aunt Ann turns the engine off and they coast along.

'Just as well we know our way about,' Aunt Ann says as they pass two men taking down signposts.

'You don't really think there'll be an invasion?' Aunt Edwina asks.

Laura can tell from the way she asks that she is not at all sure. Aunt Ann does not answer. Laura is disappointed not to be wearing her new school uniform; the dress from Berlin she has on is getting a bit short for her.

It is tea time when they arrive at the school, which takes up three buildings in a Queen Anne Crescent. They walk up a short path to the front door of the middle house, and Aunt Edwina pulls the brass bell. A fat smiling woman opens the door, a fat grey and white cat streaks out past her.

'George, George, come back at once, you naught boy!'

'Hallo, Vera. Still keeping the school well fed?' Aunt Edwina says, laughing.

'I do my bit! They're expecting you in the drawing room,' Vera says. 'Sorry about the cat,' and then, looking at Laura, 'So this is our other little refugee girl!'

That phrase *again*. Maybe if she'd had her school uniform on, she would not be called that?

There are three women in the drawing room. The eldest, who has three rows of beads dangling over her bosom, stretches out her hand.

'How nice to meet you, Laura,' she says, and Laura only just stops herself from bobbing a curtsy. You don't do that in England.

'This is Miss Thomas,' Aunt Edwina says and then, turning to one of the others, 'And this is Miss Elizabeth.'

Miss Elizabeth says, 'Hallo there,' and smiles warmly. Laura likes her at once. She is wearing pointy shoes a bit like the ones her granny wears.

'And this is Matron.' Miss Thomas introduces the third woman in the room. 'We call her Mademoiselle. She looks after all of you!'

''Allo thair, Laura my dear,' Mademoiselle says. She says hallo without an h but it does not sound like Cockney. And she says *Lowra* in the German way.

'Mademoiselle comes from Switzerland,' Miss Thomas says and goes on with a sigh, 'I don't suppose we'll be able to take the girls to Lausanne next summer, with this awful war going on!'

It's all right to be Swiss, Laura thinks, *but not German – and Jewish?*

'Never mind about that now,' Miss Elizabeth says. 'Let's get this young lady settled in!'

'She's a good settler,' Aunt Ann says and bends down to press sixpence into Laura's hand.

'You're to have sixpence pocket money a week,' she says.

13

As she leaves the drawing room with the Swiss Matron, Laura hears Miss Thomas ask how good her English is. She is proud to hear Aunt Ann say, 'Surprisingly good. She's got a lively brain; she'll be a credit to the school.'

Mademoiselle tells Laura she has been put in the bird room. Laura has no idea what that means until she sees the wallpaper with swallows swooping up and down the pale orange frieze. How nice!

'We sought you'd like to be in ze same room as our ozair little refugee, Traudl. She's from Vienna; you can speak German togezair.'

Laura does not want to speak German; it's the language of the enemy now, isn't it? Then she remembers one of the last things her grandpa said to her: *Don't forget your mother tongue.* No, of course she will not forget, but for now... For now, Laura turns her head away from Traudl, who is unpacking her case. She will *not* speak German to her; don't people know that Austrian German sounds quite different? Two English girls, Molly and Betty, are also unpacking. Laura smiles at them and they smile back; then they turn to each other and giggle.

In the mornings after breakfast they go for a walk along the seafront in 'croc', two by two. Laura is expected to walk with Traudl; they do not talk to each other. Quite soon Traudl gets moved out of the bird room and a girl called Sheila has that bed instead. So now Laura is with three English girls. She does not feel so different from them, except when Mademoiselle, who takes them for French, says 'Isn't Lowra clever! She 'as only just learnt English and now she is doing so well in French!' She hates the way the others stare at her. Laura does not want to be clever; she wants to be like them.

At needlework, which Miss Ingram takes on Saturday

mornings, Laura is worse than the others. She enjoys choosing scraps of stuff on which to try out different kinds of stitches, but they have to be very neat and even to earn a *Nicely done* from Miss Ingram. More often than not Laura gets to hear *Try another row of chain stitch* or *What a lazy buttonhole!* Miss Ingram has dark sallow skin, dark brown eyes and grey hair, which she does up in peculiar sausages. Sheila whispers to Laura that Miss Ingram is half Indian. How does she know that? Sheila says it's obvious. Laura shrugs her shoulders. Is it obvious she is half Jewish? half German? Sheila also says that everyone new sooner or later gets called into Miss Ingram's room for a heart-to-heart chat.

Eventually Laura gets called. After the preliminary *How are you getting on* kind of remarks and a rather stale chocolate biscuit, Miss Ingram gazes earnestly at her.

'You know, child, you have it in you to make everybody happy, a great and precious gift!'

Laura wriggles uncomfortably. How could Miss Ingram possibly know something like that about her? And it isn't true: she didn't make Traudl feel happy, did she? She is relieved when, after a little pat on the head, Miss Ingram tells her to run along.

Laura is chosen for the junior inter-schools gym competition. She has always been quite good at headstands and handstands, somersaults – she can do eight in a row. Hanging upside down from the wall bars is fun; climbing a rope is harder, but she makes herself do it. The hardest thing, though, is balancing on the bar; it's like walking the plank, and you have to do it without wobbling. She feels sicker and sicker as the bar gets raised higher and higher. Yes, yes, yes, she *will* do it!

One morning, a week before the competition, she wakes up to find all her bedclothes on the floor and matron bending over her with a concerned expression.

'Lowra, dear, are you all right?'

'You were sleepwalking,' Sheila says.

'You were trying to balance on the bed rail,' Molly says.

''Ave you evair walked in your sleep before?' matron asks.

Laura shakes her head. Everyone thinks it is too much of a strain for her to be in the competition. Another girl takes her place. Laura watches her school win and claps hard.

On the last day of term, packing day, they sing *Hills of the North Rejoice* at prayers, yelling the line *Shout while ye journey home* at the top of their voices. Laura can see Miss Elizabeth, who takes prayers, smiling. *Home!* Laura cannot help still thinking *home* is her granny and grandpa's large flat in the Friedrichstrasse in Berlin where she lived for five years after her parents were divorced. She remembers the year Chanukah and Christmas coincided – they lit candles on the Menorah in the drawing room and then moved into the study to light candles on the Christmas tree. That was before the Nazis made them move into a smaller flat in a Jewish district. Laura does not remember that flat nearly so well; it never became home.

She wonders if there will be a Christmas tree at Meadow House. The others have been talking about holly and ivy and giggling about mistletoe which Laura has never seen. They are all expecting a stocking filled with little presents on Christmas morning. She has made felt egg cosies for the honorary aunts, as well as one for her mother in her favourite colour, royal blue. But even as she was making it, Laura was afraid Ruth would only pretend to like it, which is why the buttonhole stitching is not very even.

Aunt Ann picks Laura up from school and on the drive to Meadow House tells her to expect a big surprise. The surprise turns out to be that Ruth is already there, her arms stretched out wide as Laura comes through the front door. Laura wishes she were as pleased as the grown-ups expect her to be.

'You're in the spare room this time,' Aunt Ann says.

It's because my mother isn't their housemaid any longer, so we don't have to be in the servants' room, Laura thinks.

When she wakes up on Christmas morning she sees a bulging grey stocking with sprigs of holly sticking out of it dangling at the end of her bed. *Good,* she thinks, *I've got one like the others.* She unwraps the little packages; is very pleased with the box of crayons, the India rubber, bar of lavender soap, three red and white marbles, a whipped-cream walnut and, in the toe of the stocking, a piece of coal.

'Vot's zat for?' Ruth asks. Then she gives Laura three handkerchiefs with a blue L embroidered in the corner.

'It's not much, dahlink, but it's viz all my love,' and she strokes Laura's hair. Laura wishes her mother would not say things like that. She gives her the royal blue egg cosy. Ruth looks at it with her head on one side.

'An egg cosy,' Laura says.

'I sink it's a nose varmer,' Ruth says and slips it over her nose. Laura smiles a bit.

At breakfast the honorary aunts explain that the piece of coal is for luck. Laura gives them their egg cosies.

'What's this, my lamb?' Aunt Edwina asks.

Laura goes pink with pleasure. Being called *my lamb* is almost as good as her granny calling her *my little goldfinch.*

'Purple is my favourite colour,' Aunt Tessa says.

'So beautifully stitched,' Aunt Ann says.

'I have a blue one,' Ruth says, 'but I sink zey are nose varmers!' And she slips hers on her nose again.

The three old ladies smile a bit; Laura looks into her lap. Aunt Edwina turns to Laura.

'We don't have a Christmas tree, but after breakfast you

and I will go into the garden and pick the first Christmas roses to put on the table for lunch!'

Barney comes with them wearing his new blue and green plaid coat, which Aunt Tessa has given him because he is getting quite old and shivers in the wind. The Christmas roses look lovely on the table.

There are visitors for lunch: Mr. Pocklington with his little boy Matthew – Aunt Ann has explained that poor Mr. Pocklington lost his wife when Matthew was born. And there is also Miss Martha Dearlove who lives by herself in the cottage up the lane. When she arrives, Laura does not think she has a *dear love* kind of face: it is too pointy and her grey hair is done up in a tight bun. Laura sees her mother look up expectantly at Mr. Pocklington. When they sit down to lunch he talks about the windy weather; a new bird-feeder he has found which the squirrels have not yet mastered; that his golf course is likely to be turned into pasture and, with a delighted smile, that Matthew will be going to school in January. Laura sees Ruth's interest waning. She tries to talk to Matthew who is sitting next to her, but he does not respond, just crams forkfuls of turkey, sprouts and potato into his mouth. Martha Dearlove talks, almost regretfully, about the fact that in spite of what they were told to expect, there have not been any air raids; and that the evacuees in South Petherton are making a nuisance of themselves.

'Poor mites,' Mr. Pocklington says.

Laura is gratified to know that English evacuees can be *poor mites* as well as refugees. Mr. Pocklington does not seem to think that *she* is *a poor mite*. After lunch, he asks her to look after his little Matthew. She shows him the three marbles she had in her stocking.

'Oh, look, Matthew, they're splendid oxblood ones,' Mr. Pocklington says, but Matthew is not very responsive. Laura did not know they were called that.

They go for a short walk across the fields to see Martha Dearlove back to her cottage. Mr. Pocklington carries Matthew on his shoulders; Laura remembers how her father used to do that when she was younger. Ruth does not come with them, she has a headache.

At teatime Laura likes the marzipan icing on the cake better than the cake itself but she knows she has to eat it all. Her granny used to say: *Eat everything on your plate and the sun will shine tomorrow!* The honorary aunts say nothing of the kind, but Laura knows what is expected of her. She likes the way hardly anyone ever says *You must... you mustn't... you ought to...* And yet ground rules are quite clear.

Ruth has reappeared.

'You look well rested, my dear. Your cheeks are quite rosy!'

Laura knows Ruth has put on rouge. Can't Aunt Ann tell?

They play a card game called *Red Nines* with two packs of cards. Matthew is allowed to win. Laura minds a bit, but then she is rather proud to think that she is not the youngest at the table.

Next day, Boxing Day – Aunt Ann explains why it is called that – there is a Quaker picnic a few miles away.

'A picnic? On a freezing day like zis?' Ruth looks out of the window at the grey sky and branches bending in the wind.

'It's quite a sheltered spot; we go every year, come wind, come weather!' Aunt Ann says.

Come wind, come weather. Laura thinks it sounds like the beginning of a poem.

'You are not obliged to come,' Aunt Tessa looks at Ruth rather sternly. Laura bends down to fasten Barney's lead on his collar.

'Zen I stay here,' Ruth says. Her *here* sounds like *hier*,

Laura thinks, without being able to explain the difference to herself.

Aunt Ann gives Laura a bag of pink and white marshmallows to carry.

'We'll toast them over the bonfire, after these,' and she holds up strings of chipolata sausages.

There is quite a crowd when they get to the picnic spot which is down a steep path. People are throwing twigs on the bonfire, holding their hands over it and stamping their feet.

'You can hand the marshmallows round now,' Aunt Ann tells Laura. She recognises the girl called Penelope who visited Meadow House. They say hallo but Laura does not think Penelope is very pleased to see her.

'Sit down here with us, my dear,' a woman who is probably Penelope's mother says. Laura sees Aunt Ann waving so she runs back to her.

'That's the refugee girl,' she hears Penelope tell her mother.

'I know, you might have made more of an effort with her, Penny!'

Laura does not want people to make an effort with her; she wants them to *like* her. She toasts a pink marshmallow. It tastes delicious, but she is not quite sure whether all the kind people sitting round the fire are only nodding and smiling at her because she is a refugee.

Ruth goes back to London the next day. Laura wishes she were not pleased her mother has left – but she is. She can't wait for school to start again.

When she gets back, it is freezing cold in the form rooms; they take it in turns to warm their bottoms in front of the anthracite stoves. In English they are reading an abridged version of *Ivanhoe* with Miss Elizabeth. Most of the others think it is boring, but Laura reads on well ahead of where they have got to in class. Every day between the end of prep and supper there is an hour's free time. She takes *Ivanhoe* into the library and sits at the table covered with a tapestry cloth with long tassels that reminds her of one her granny and grandpa had. There is very little news from them now, or from her father, but Laura feels them safe inside herself. She knows they love her.

She wants to know whether Ivanhoe will marry Rowena or Rebecca; she so wants him to marry Rebecca, but in her heart she knows it will be Rowena. When he does, Laura feels as if he has turned her down personally. It was never good to be Jewish, was it? Why wasn't it? Laura shuts the book and stays in the library for a while. She is usually by herself, but surrounded by books she does not feel alone. Before *Ivanhoe* she read *Alice in Wonderland* in English; she already knows the story. She loves the Tenniel illustrations, and her favourite bit is the Mad Hatter's tea party. *Twinkle, twinkle little bat, / How I wonder what you're at, / Like a tea tray in the sky / Up above the world you fly!* She laughs out loud as she walks across to the dining room with the gong for supper clanging. You can't translate that into German! She has written a composition about the Mad Hatter. As she was writing, she found she was not only describing him but making him up in a new way as she went along. Miss Elizabeth asked her to read it out and to her delight everyone laughed.

She sits down in the dining room opposite the large reproduction of the *Mona Lisa*. The housekeeper Vera claps her hands for them to stop talking.

'Girls, you know food is being rationed because of the war. We won't starve, but there is going to be less of everything. Now I was thinking that if everyone gave up sugar in their tea, then cook could go on making her delicious puddings. Hands up everyone who is willing to do that!'

Everyone, staff and girls, puts up their hands.

Vera smiles. 'That's settled then!'

Every Saturday morning there is a letter from Ruth. Holding the unopened envelope makes Laura feel like the others; everyone gets post from their parents once a week, but when she has taken the letter out of its envelope she feels lost. It smells of cigarette smoke and is written partly in English, partly in German. She has not yet seen the furnished room into which her mother has recently moved. Ruth has stopped being a housemaid, has got a job as a waitress – a nippy in a Lyons Cornerhouse. In the last letter Ruth told her that she is to spend half the Easter holidays in London and half in Meadow House.

Laura travels to London with Molly, whose parents are picking her up at Paddington. Ruth is taking the day off from Lyons so she can meet the train. The closer they get to London, the more Laura hopes Molly's parents and her mother will not meet. Molly is hanging out of the window as the train pulls into the station.

'I can see them, I can see them,' she shouts and is out of the train in a flash.

Laura steps on to the platform. Yes, there is Ruth hurrying towards her, wearing the black felt hat that looked just right in Berlin, but here it looks sort of... Then Laura is caught up in a hug and for a few seconds everything is all right. When Ruth lets go, she looks round – Molly and her parents have disappeared. Good.

There is just enough space for two beds in the room in Golders Green. There is a sink and a gas ring behind a bead curtain. The little table by the window is laid for two. There are Frankfurters with potato salad for lunch, chocolate pudding for afters.

'I saved some sugar,' Ruth says.

Laura is just about to say that everyone at school has given up sugar in their tea when she feels her cheek being stroked. Ruth gazes at her. 'Vell, is it nice to be viz your muzzer?'

The words get stuck inside Laura; all she can see are her mother's bright red fingernails. So instead of talking about sugar, she asks, 'When am I going to Somerset?'

Ruth's eyes fill with tears. They finish their meal in silence. Later on, going for a walk in Golders Hill Park, things relax a little. Then they go to see a Betty Grable film. Laura enjoys the Technicolor: she has not been to many films in colour, only some cartoons her father took her to in Berlin. Before they go to bed, Laura sees Ruth swallow some pills.

'Zey help me sleep,' she says.

Laura wishes they did not have to sleep in the same room and wishes she did not have to go downstairs to the bathroom, which might be engaged. Before she slips into her bed, Ruth bends over her and kisses her.

'You're all I have now,' she whispers. It makes Laura feel uncomfortable to hear her mother say that.

They have cornflakes for breakfast.

'Ve're quite English, aren't ve,' Ruth says with a grin. She has rearranged her shifts at the Cornerhouse so she will only be working from four to nine.

'Today you come viz me, and ze Belgian vill stay viz you!'

'The Belgian?'

When they get to Marble Arch, the Belgian turns out to be a tall man in khakis. He gives Ruth a smacking kiss and is about to do the same for Laura but she backs away from him.

'Zis is Louis,' Ruth says and disappears.

Louis finds a table near the band and orders a knickerbocker glory for Laura and a cup of tea for himself.

'Coffee 'ere is undrinkable,' he says. He sounds a bit like

Mademoiselle at school.

Ruth, changed into her nippy's uniform, brings their order. Laura barely recognises her mother. She digs the long spoon right down into the knickerbocker glory. After about an hour Louis leaves.

'Your mozair is a grand leetle voman,' he says and pinches Laura's cheek. She disappears right inside herself. Presently, Ruth reappears with a piece of chocolate gâteau.

'You stay here and read, dahlink!'

Laura gets out *Little Women* and forgets where she is.

Back in the Golders Green room, Ruth is sitting on Louis's knee. Laura wonders when he will go; she is very tired. When he finally leaves, Laura hears him ask Ruth how long her daughter is staying. Laura longs to be with Barney in Meadow House.

'Now you know a bit of my life,' Ruth says as she kisses her goodbye at Paddington. She sees Laura into the compartment and does not get out until the guard is slamming the doors.

'I shall miss you, dahlink!' Ruth calls as the train pulls out. Laura does not believe her.

It is easy to talk to the honorary aunts; they understand about the Mad Hatter and Ivanhoe. They enquire with great concern about Ruth.

'She's a waitress in Lyons now.'

Laura does not mention Louis.

'That must be hard work,' they say.

They go for long walks with Barney. Laura learns to identify wild flowers with nice names like Herb Robert and Red Campion. Woody Nightshade is poisonous. There are some tiny pink berries called spindleberries with bright orange seeds inside; you can't eat them.

'I don't suppose your mother has news from Berlin?' Aunt Ann asks.

Laura shakes her head; she does not want to think about Berlin. She listens to Children's Hour with Auntie Doris and Uncle Mac. She loves it when he says *Goodnight children!* And after a tiny pause adds *Everywhere!* Then she wonders if he really means *everywhere* or only England.

Back at school everyone is talking about what they did in the holidays.

'My Dad took me and my brother to…'

'We went to see my granny and grandpa…'

'I had a new bike for my birthday…'

'I'm going to have a baby brother or sister in a few weeks time…'

'We had a family reunion, hundreds of cousins, most of them got leave, only the one in the navy wasn't there…'

When they look at Laura she says, 'I had a knickerbocker glory in a Lyons Cornerhouse!' She explains about the Cornerhouse. They don't know what she is not telling them.

She feels hungry all the time, but she does not like to mention it, because none of the others do; she realises how much more important food was in Berlin. She loved discussing what they were going to eat and going shopping with her granny, the fun of trying out new recipes like making waffles with a waffle iron. She longs constantly for sweet things. At breakfast, they have margarine and marmite on their bread; on Sundays there is toast and marmalade, one spoonful each. Laura knows quite well it means a teaspoonful, but one Sunday morning she takes a dessertspoonful – no one has actually ever said anything about it being a teaspoon. No one says anything now. So that's all right then? When she says something to her neighbour at the table, the girl turns her head away. When, a bit later, she asks Molly something while they are making their beds (with hospital corners), she starts talking to one of the others. On Monday, when she asks to borrow a rubber, it is as if everyone has gone deaf. Lessons go on as usual; the teachers do not leave Laura out when they ask questions, but none of the girls speaks to her. Not Tuesday, not Wednesday, Thursday or Friday – not even on Saturday, when they sit round the dining room table doing needlework. So on Sunday when the marmalade is passed round, Laura does not take any. As soon as the pot of marmalade has passed on to the next girl, her neighbour smiles at her and says something about the hockey match on the coming Friday. Later on, Molly comes up to her. 'How did you like being sent to Coventry?' she asks. Oh, so that's what it was!

Sometimes they are allowed into the drawing room for the six o'clock news; they sit on the carpet and listen to Bruce Belfrage or Alvar Liddell reading it. Winston Churchill is the new Prime Minister, and there is a coalition government. Laura remembers talk about that at Meadow House. Towards the end of May there is bad news: our troops are stuck in Dunkirk. Laura thinks *our* quite spontaneously. They have looked Dunkirk up on the map in geography – it is very near, just across the Channel. One or two girls have fathers there. They hear how everyone who has a boat, however small, is setting out for Dunkirk; the boats go there and back, again and again, picking up as many men as they can. When Laura hears they are rescuing dogs as well, she cries. Some girls are knitting scarves and balaclava helmets for our boys. Laura can knit quite well – her granny taught her in Berlin – but she knits the German way, which wouldn't do for our boys, would it! So she pretends she can't knit.

At prayers in the morning she closes her eyes and asks God to forgive her for telling lies. She wonders if it really matters and thinks of all those millions of people asking God for different things. Who is He supposed to listen to? When the bit about *Through Jesus Christ our Lord* comes at the end of the Lord's Prayer, Laura listens away (like one *looks* away). Jesus is not for her, He is for the others. She does not go to church on Sundays with everyone else because her mother has asked that she should not. In case she turns into a Christian? Not that Ruth ever goes to synagogue now.

'Not ze same wizout ze parents,' she tells Laura. Perhaps Ruth has stopped believing in God?

Laura hides herself away in the library when the others put on their royal blue Sunday coats and black velour hats to go to church. She meets them outside after the service to go for the walk; she feels she is somehow cheating to be wearing the royal blue coat when she has not been to church. There is never anyone left to walk with, so she has to walk with the mistress on duty.

The following holidays, Ruth has moved to a different room in Golders Green. It is a bit bigger than the last one, and they have their own bathroom. There is a different man, too; the Belgian has disappeared.

'Vell, he is in ze army…' is all Ruth says.

The new man has red hair and is called Erich, though he prefers the English version Eric. He lives quite close by.

'Intelligent chep, setting up his own electrical business,' Ruth says.

Laura does not much like him – perhaps he does not much like her? At least her mother does not sit on his knee. She has stopped being a nippy at Lyons and now works in a small munitions factory.

'Making bombs to kill zat beast,' she says, meaning Hitler.

Laura has brought Palgrave's *Golden Treasury* to show

Ruth; she knows quite a few of the poems by heart. When she starts on 'The Lady of Shalott', she can see Ruth is not really listening, even though she says 'Lovely, dahlink' every time Laura stops for breath.

'Ve'll take you to a show,' Ruth promises.

Laura wants to see *Macbeth*. They are doing it at school, and she has been reading the part of the First Witch.

'Macbess?' her mother asks.

Laura nods hopefully.

'Without me,' Eric grunts.

Laura looks away from him. She really wants to see it.

'Zen I take my daughter by myself!' Ruth says.

So she does love me a bit, Laura thinks. Their brown eyes meet.

After the play, it is good to get back to the Golders Green room without Eric there. Ruth puts the kettle on and gets out some alphabet biscuits called *Russian Bread*, which Laura has no seen since Berlin. She dips her L-shaped biscuit into the topaz coloured tea and sucks it; her mother does the same with her R. They smile at each other and Laura feels confident enough to say, 'I don't really like Eric!'

She does not have to see him much more: he is being interned on the Isle of Man with the other enemy aliens. *Collar the lot*, Churchill has said. Ruth is outraged.

'Zey sink ve are Nazis? Vy zey sink ve came to zis country?'

Almost every night the sirens go, and they rush into the damp Anderson shelter at the bottom of the garden with the other tenants in the house huddling together as the bombs crash and the anti-aircraft guns respond. Laura is not frightened: she knows, though she does not know *how* she knows, that she will not be hurt. *The News Chronicle* carries photographs of bombed out people outside smouldering houses; the number of dead is not yet known. Churchill broadcasts again. *We shall not flag... we shall never surrender...* Laura so much wants to be included in that *we.*

The war goes on and on.

We survive the Battle of Britain.

We lug our gasmasks about and occasionally try them on.

We make do and mend, darn socks, patch elbows, tie knots in our knicker elastic when it wears out, because you cannot buy any new.

We take our baths in five inches of water and wash with one bar of soap a month.

We eat our reconstituted egg and Spam.

We allow iron railings to be removed and give up saucepans, to be turned into munitions.

We know that careless talk costs lives.

We welcome the Americans into the war as our allies after the Japanese bomb Pearl Harbor.

We hear with dismay that Hong Kong has surrendered to the Japanese.

We welcome the Russians as our allies when the Germans invade their country.

We grieve when Singapore falls to the Japanese.

We are jubilant when General Montgomery defeats Rommel at El Alamein.

§

Laura has just passed her thirteenth birthday. She goes on spending half her holidays with her mother, half with the honorary aunts in Somerset. But it is at school she feels most at ease.

When they go out for their walks in croc along the seafront after breakfast and before tea, they pass convalescing wounded servicemen in bright blue suits and red ties, some limping along on crutches, some with only one arm, some with a black patch over an eye. They always wave at the girls, and the girls wave back. *They can't tell I'm not English*, Laura thinks.

One night there is an air raid. German bombers on their way back from Bristol unload what bombs they have left on Weston-super-Mare. As soon as the siren goes, everyone rushes downstairs in their pyjamas, gasmask boxes slung across their shoulders. The air raid wardens have declared the basement of the school building even safer than the air raid shelters. It is quite fun seeing the staff appear in their nightwear; Matron has her hair down, and where are Miss Owen's teeth? You can see nearly all of Miss Hetherington's bosom because her dressing gown barely covers it. Miss Dutton is tapping the air, playing a spectral piano. Miss Thomas and Miss Elizabeth, one in a brown, the other in a blue-checked dressing gown, look composed, their hair tidy, teeth in place. Cook hands round lime green lemonade, made with powder crystals. There are also Garibaldi biscuits called squashed flies. Matron calls the register; they are all present and correct. The raid goes on longer than usual; there are loud thuds making the building shake. Molly, who is a weekly boarder and lives quite close to the school, has gone pale. Laura puts an arm round her. 'It'll be all right!'

At last the All Clear sounds. As they file back upstairs, there is a lurid glow against the windows. They pull back the curtains and see their town in flames. There is a screech of fire engines.

'Oh my God, I think that's our house!' Molly screams.

Laura puts an arm round her again. Molly pushes her away. 'I suppose you're pleased, you Jerry!' she yells.

Laura cannot believe her ears.

Miss Elizabeth is standing behind them. 'Time for everyone to get back to bed, quick as you can now!'

She turns to Molly. 'We will telephone your parents first thing in the morning, my dear.' But it is on Laura's shoulder that Miss Elizabeth has put her hand.

Back in her bed, Laura whispers the Hebrew prayer her granny used to say with her, but not the German one. In the morning Molly comes up to her.

'I'm really sorry,' she says 'I didn't mean it. I've just spoken to my parents. The incendiaries missed our house!'

'Oh, it's all right,' Laura says. But is it?

Miss Elizabeth gets Laura to come to her in the morning room. She takes her pince-nez off her nose and wipes it.

Then she says, 'Miss Tate tells me she has discovered a refugee doctor and his wife from Berlin who have settled in the town; it turns out his wife knew your mother. So we've got in touch with them, and Mrs. Karlsberg has said she will read some German literature with you. They've invited you to tea next Saturday.'

After a moment Miss Elizabeth adds, 'The war won't go on forever, you know, and it won't do for you to forget your mother tongue, will it?'

Exactly what her grandpa said.

The Karlsbergs live the other end of Weston. The letter Laura has from her mother that morning mentions that Hannah was one of the brainy ones at the Luisenschule in Berlin. With the breeze blowing in her face, Laura walks along the front expectantly, pleased that she, like a good many of the others, has been invited out for tea. Some of the girls go riding on a Saturday; Laura waves to them as they canter past on the sands.

She finds the Karlsbergs' house quite easily and when the door opens, there is a small woman with greying hair and large brown eyes who holds her hand out and says, 'You don't look very like your mother!' Then, after a moment, stroking Laura's cheeks, 'Well may be, a little, after all, round the eyes!' Her English is fluent, much better than Ruth's, but the intonation is German.

In the sitting room Dr. Klaus Karlsberg, a small round man with friendly eyes, shakes Laura's hand, asks how old she is, how she likes her school and whether she can still speak German.

'Ja, ja, ein Bisschen!'

After tea he disappears, and Hannah Karlsberg gets out a copy of Schiller's *Maria Stuart*.

'We'll take it in turns to read. Stop and ask if there's anything you don't understand.' Suddenly Laura realises Hannah is speaking German to her. They sit next to each other on the sofa. At the end of Act I, Hannah closes the book.

'That's enough for today. Did you enjoy it?'

Yes, Laura has enjoyed it. Then, to her surprise, she finds herself telling Hannah about the test she had to take with MD children at the elementary school in Northolt before war broke out. She has not talked about that anyone else.

'Well, I'm sure you passed that all right!' They laugh together. 'You'll come again next Saturday? And remember me to your mother when you write to her, won't you!'

Ruth has moved from Golders Green to a room in a large house in Muswell Hill. They have to share a bathroom again, but to Laura's delight there is a small room of her own with wallpaper that has illustrations of John Gilpin careering about on a horse. When she asks about Eric, Ruth tells her he has been released from the internment camp and has joined the Pioneer Corps, where he spends a good deal of time peeling potatoes. There does not seem to be another man about. While Ruth is out at the munitions factory with her hair tied up in a turban, Laura enjoys time by herself reading *Emma* and learning Tennyson's poem 'The Revenge' by heart. She is going in for a verse speaking competition at school.

Very occasionally there is post from friends in Switzerland. The news is sad: the grandparents have been deported to Theresienstadt, Laura's father is still in Berlin, *working hard* the friends write. They do not say what he is working at. One morning during that holiday the postman brings another letter from Switzerland. In it there is a red printed card from Theresienstadt which Laura's granny has signed *Widow*. Now they know that her grandpa is dead. Ruth and Laura stand hand in hand looking at the grandparents' photographs on the bedside table. They do not cry.

The next day, Ruth runs a temperature. Her left ear hurts badly. Laura goes down to the pay phone in the hall to let the factory know Ruth cannot come to work. The person she speaks to tells her to make sure Ruth brings a doctor's certificate when she comes back to work. Laura does not know whether Ruth has a doctor. Mrs. Wilson, their landlady, comes out into the hall.

'I couldn't help overhearing what you were saying, dear. I'm sorry your mother's not well. Let me know if she'd like a doctor. Our Dr. Jackson will come if necessary.'

She smiles at Laura.

'How do you like your little room with the Caldecott wallpaper?'

Laura has no idea who or what Caldecott is.

Ruth's ear gets worse. Dr. Jackson comes. Yes, the ear is quite bad; she will have to stay in bed a few days until her temperature has gone down.

'You'll look after her?' Dr. Jackson gives Laura a prescription. 'Get these from the chemist. She's to take them three times a day.'

He shakes Laura's hand and promises to look in again.

When the doctor has gone, Ruth says, 'Dahlink, I'm sorry, I spoil your holidays!'

Laura knows it is the red card from Theresienstadt that is spoiling the holidays.

'Give me a kiss,' Ruth says, and Laura kisses her mother's hot forehead.

'Mrs. Wilson's nice, isn't she?' Laura says.

'And Mr. Wilson,' Ruth says.

On her way out to the chemist, Laura sees Mr. and Mrs. Wilson dressed in Victorian clothes; Mrs. Wilson is all in purple, setting off her snow white hair, and Mr. Wilson looks dapper in a black velvet jacket and mauve cravat. They wave to Laura and explain they are film extras about to go out on a shoot. Laura feels quite excited; none of the others at school live in a house with film extras.

She does not mind looking after her mother: she enjoys going to the chemist and doing the shopping with Ruth's ration book. At the grocer she gets a small piece of Cheddar cheese and a tin of pilchards in tomato sauce, on points.

'Eggs are in,' the assistant says and gives Laura a large brown one.

She would like to buy her mother a bunch of flowers, but she dare not spend any extra money. She hurries back home. What a lot of different meanings *home* has come to have! She likes the Wilsons' house best of the places her mother has lived.

When she gets back in, Ruth is asleep. Her cheeks are flushed and her breath rasps. Laura boils the egg carefully for three minutes on one of the two gas rings in the recess by the window.

When Ruth wakes up, Laura gives her the pills and says with some pride, 'I've boiled an egg for you.'

'And you?' Ruth asks, 'Vot vill you have?'

There is a knock on the door. Mrs. Wilson comes in with a thermos flask of soup. She is back in ordinary clothes, but there is still some pinkish make-up on her face. She has also brought a pile of American film magazines.

'These'll while away the time,' she says and, looking at Laura, 'You managing all right, dear?'

Laura nods. It is quite a relief to know there is a grown-up about.

Ruth gets a bit better every day. Dr. Jackson tells Laura she is a good little nurse. Mrs. Wilson goes on bringing hot soup and stays to chat.

When she finds out it is Laura's birthday in a day or two, she says, 'We'll have to see what we can do about that, won't we?'

On the day, both Mr. and Mrs. Wilson come quite early. They give Laura a large tin of Libby's asparagus with half a crown taped to it.

'Happy Birthday – these are pre-war! Have a lovely day, my dear. We can't stay long; there's another shoot this morning. Elizabethan dress this time, takes me hours to get into that doublet and hose!' Mr. Wilson smiles at Laura.

'Vot a couple!' Ruth says with admiration when they have gone.

The Wilsons are different kind of English again – not like the Somerset honorary aunts or Miss Elizabeth, nor like Cockney Arthur and his parents. There is a kind of gloss about the way they speak.

Ruth says she feels well enough to go out and choose a present for Laura.

'Vot vould you like?'

'A poetry book,' Laura says and sees her mother's eyes glaze over.

'If zat's vot you really vant...'

'Let's go to Bumpus's!'

'Vair?'

Miss Elizabeth has told Laura about that famous book-shop in Oxford Street. On the bus, Laura hopes Ruth will not talk because she sounds so foreign. In fact, she hardly opens her mouth – perhaps she knows what Laura is feeling? Laura hooks her arm through her mother's by way of silent apology for her thoughts.

'Is your ear still hurting?'

'No, much better, sank you, but I was sinking about...' Ruth does not go on to say what she was thinking about. Birthday celebrations in Berlin, perhaps?

In Bumpus's Laura forgets everything except books. She loves the smell of fresh print even though the paper in the new books is not quite white and has speckles in it. But the dark blue Oxford poetry editions on India paper are there in pre-war splendour – Keats, Byron, Shelley. Laura hesitates. She takes Shelley off the shelf; it falls open at 'Ozymandias'. She knows that by heart. Yes, she'll have Shelley for her birthday.

'It's five shillings,' she says shyly, 'but I can put my half crown towards it!'

'You keep zat,' Ruth tells her. 'I pay! You looked after me so nice!'

When they get back to Muswell Hill, they open the tin of asparagus, which is quite delicious. As they get up to clear the table, Laura notices with a start that she is now taller than her mother. She takes *The Complete Works* of Shelley to bed and reads 'Ode to the West Wind'. Then, before she falls asleep, she looks at some of Mrs. Wilson's film magazines; photographs of those handsome men and beautiful girls in evening dress or bathing suits kissing each other make her feel quite woozy. It has been a good birthday – better than she expected.

She spends the rest of the holidays at Meadow House. The honorary aunts are not as cheerful as usual. Neither is Barney – he is not in the hall to welcome Laura. He lies in his basket in the kitchen and only just manages to wag his tail when he sees her.

'He's over eighteen years old,' Aunt Ann says.

'We think the time may have come...' Aunt Edwina says

'We'll take him to the vet in a day or two,' Aunt Tessa says.

'Just a whiff of gas and then it's all over; he won't know a thing,' Aunt Ann says.

'It's the kindest thing. Then we'll bury him in the garden,' Aunt Edwina says.

On the morning they are about to take Barney to the vet, Laura goes to the dining room sideboard where a box of Black Magic chocolates is kept to offer visitors. She knows Barney adores chocolates, the soft ones – he does not have many teeth left. She picks out the orange cream, the strawberry cream and the coffee cream; feels his tongue warm and wet on her hand. He goes on looking at her, hoping for more.

Ben the gardener digs a rectangular hole under one of the apple trees at the far end of the garden. Laura looks away as they put Barney's body in it; she does no want to see him dead. When the hole is covered with earth, they go indoors and Aunt Tessa gets out photographs of Barney as a puppy.

Laura has not yet told the honorary aunts about the card from Theresienstadt. She will wait until Aunt Ann asks if there is any news; she always does. But the days pass: they do a large jigsaw of the British Isles with county shaped pieces; they collect horse dung from the field next to the garden; they listen to the Brains Trust with Dr. Joad squeaking on about it all depending what you mean by whatever the subject happens to be – quite often something like the mating habits of the greater crested grebe, about which Julian Huxley is astonishingly knowledgeable and Commander Campbell reassuringly matter-of-fact.

The last day of the holidays comes, but still Aunt Ann has not enquired about family news. Perhaps they expect Laura to tell them without being asked? So after supper – the box of Black Magic has been passed round, no one seeming to notice that any chocolates are missing – Laura mentions the red card from Theresienstadt.

'It's all quite dreadful!' Aunt Ann says and strokes her head.

'Your grandfather should have been allowed to die at home in his bed!' Aunt Edwina says.

'You must remember him as you knew him!' Aunt Tessa says.

Laura feels all three of them looking at her with pity. She cannot bear that; she does not want to be pitiable.

Summer term passes pleasantly. There is tennis coaching, though Laura has to admit to herself she enjoys the idea of it better than the reality – she is not much good at getting the ball across the net, let alone making it go where she wants to. She is better at swimming, loves that sensation of total immersion, floating on her back from one end of the pool to the other; then the tingle of coolness inside and outside her body as she dries herself.

Her breasts are growing, not as big as some of the other girls', but still they're beginning to show even when she has clothes on. She wishes her hair was curly or at least wavy; her mother's is wavy and was jet black, her father's fair and straight – hers is a sort of halfway house between that, dark brown and dead straight. You can get your hair permed but that is very expensive. Will she ever get a boyfriend with boring hair like that? For the moment, boyfriends are what other people have.

They see very few boys or men, only the gardener, who is too old to be called up, and sometimes Molly's brother, who goes to a boys' school in the town. He is allowed to call for her at weekends and, when they walk out of the front gate, everyone hangs out of the window to catch a glimpse of him – once he waves up at them; afterwards the headmistress, who must also have been looking out of the window, tells Molly it is inappropriate for her brother to do that. Then there is the elderly, stooping music master who comes on Thursdays to teach them songs to the tune of Strauss waltzes. The words are silly: *Old winter wears a garment of white...* By common consent, the poor man becomes old winter wearing white combinations; no one can keep a straight face as they sing. Occasionally, there is a plumber or an electrician or a window cleaner. some of the girls giggle when they are about, but Laura hardly notices them. Except that one day it turns out that a girl in the sixth form has taken too much notice of the window cleaner and is expelled.

'They were caught doing it! In the cellar!'

Laura is not exactly sure what *doing it* amounts to. She knows it is something you are supposed not to do until you are married, because you might have a baby, but she is hazy as to what it is that people actually do. Maybe it gives you the kind of woozy feelings she had when she was looking at Mrs. Wilson's film magazines? She listens without saying much when the others talk about where babies come from.

'Out of your bottom,' one of the girls says; she has watched her cat having kittens. Surely that can't be right? But those thoughts are not really uppermost in Laura's mind.

She looks forward to Sunday evenings when Miss Elizabeth reads to the older girls while they do embroidery. Laura is embroidering a small tablecloth with ladies in crinolines in each corner; two are going to be in mauve and two in dark purple. Aunt Edwina gave her the cloth, along with skeins of embroidery silks. Laura runs her fingers over the silks and thinks of her granny, who taught her embroidery stitches; her granny who is now... She allows the cloth to fall into her lap and listens to what Miss Elizabeth is reading. It is a sad story about a man who goes blind, *The Light that Failed* by Rudyard Kipling. Laura is always disappointed when Miss Elizabeth closes the book and says, 'That's enough for today. More next Sunday, gels!'

The term comes to a fun end with a concert in the Winter Garden, Myra Hess playing Chopin. Hess's nephew goes to the same school as Molly's brother, which is why Weston is lucky enough to have a musician who normally performs at the National Gallery in London, even when there are air raids on. It never occurs to Laura that someone must have paid for her ticket; going to something at the end of the summer term is simply what happens at school.

On prize-giving morning, Laura can hardly believe it when her name is called out – she has won a prize for excellent work in English Literature! Miss Elizabeth hands her a copy of Tennyson's *Poems,* bound in green morocco leather. Laura wishes she could tell her granny and grandpa and her father about that!

Just as she is beginning to look forward to having the first part of the long summer break in Meadow House, she is called into the drawing room where Aunt Ann, looking unusually pale, is sitting between Miss Thomas and Miss Elizabeth.

'I'm afraid there's sad news,' Miss Elizabeth says.

Immediately Laura thinks: *Now my granny has died as well as my grandpa!*

But what Aunt Ann says is, 'Our dear friend Tessa passed away last week.'

'So you'll understand,' Miss Elizabeth turns to Laura, 'that it'll be better if this summer you spend the whole holidays in London with your mother.'

'I see,' Laura is dismayed and only just manages to say, 'I'm very, very sorry about Aunt Tessa!'

Then Aunt Ann says, 'And as if we have not had enough to cope with, your mother has asked to have the things we've been storing for her – those five enormous packing cases you brought from Germany!'

Aunt Ann says it as if it was wrong of them to have brought so much. Laura remembers: those crates called *lifts*, with their linen, china, glass, silver.

'Aunt Edwina sends love,' Aunt Ann says as she is leaving. Perhaps she has noticed Laura's woebegone expression?

'We'll see you in the Christmas holidays.'

Miss Elizabeth pats Laura on the shoulder as she goes out. Those little pats have great survival value.

So while the others are chattering and laughing excitedly on packing day, Laura stuffs things into her case with a heavy heart. She does not join in with them as they yell *Shout while ye journey home* at prayers and does not fully understand why she cannot go to Meadow House, even though Aunt Tessa has died. *They don't really love me*, she thinks, *they aren't really my aunts!*

As she stands by herself in the hall, much too early, waiting for the taxi to take her to the station, Miss Elizabeth comes to wish her a happy holiday.

'We'll see you back in September. It'll be noses to the grindstone then, getting ready for School Certificate. We expect you to get Matric Exempt, you know! We want to see your name up on the honours board!'

She makes Laura wish it were September now. Yes, she wants her name up in gold letters on the honours board.

§

Ruth has moved back to Golders Green and is living with a man called Heinz or Henry whom Laura has not yet met. She wonders how she is going to pass almost two months with her mother with nothing to look forward to.

When she gets to London, she takes one look at Ruth's new man Heinz/Henry and hates him. He has steely blue eyes, thin straight lips and crinkly fairish hair scraped back from his not very high forehead. He looks her up and down in a way that makes waves of anger rise inside her.

As soon as they are sitting down to a meal of Spam and reconstituted egg with bought potato salad, he says to her, 'You'll be pleased to hear your mother's found a nice little holiday job for you!' He speaks fluent English with that grating German intonation Laura cannot bear.

She looks at her mother. 'But...but... I've brought a lot of revision reading; it's school cert next year; I want to get Matric Exempt because...'

She cannot tell Ruth and Henry about the honours board on which she would like to see her name. As for mentioning her literature prize, that seems totally impossible.

'My sister,' Henry says, 'was working full time in a factory at your age. And now she's got her own business in Chicago. Clever girl!'

Laura does not want her own business in Chicago; she wants Matric exempt.

'Vell, just for a month, ze last two veeks you don't have to vork.' Ruth's voice is trembling on the verge of tears.

'What job?' Laura asks.

'A little textile vorkshop; you just do ze ironing.'

'All day?'

'I expect they'll give you a lunch break!' Henry says with a sharp laugh.

'When do I have to start?' Oh, why isn't she in Somerset? Why did Aunt Tessa have to die?

'Not til Monday. Ve have ze veekend togezzer!'

Laura says nothing more. Though she is quite hungry, she does not finish the food on her plate.

'Not good enough for you? They give you caviar at that posh school of yours?' Henry is belligerent.

Laura sees Ruth give him a pleading look. He takes out a packet of Woodbines and offers Laura one.

'Go on, one won't hurt you,' Ruth says.

Laura shakes her head.

She is to sleep on the couch in the room where they have been eating and smoking. There is a door through into another room, just big enough for a double bed. The kitchen and bathroom are across the hall; they don't have to share them. It is the largest place Ruth has lived in so far, but Laura wishes they were still in Muswell Hill in the Wilsons' nice house. When Ruth comes to kiss her goodnight, Laura pushes her away. 'I think he's awful!' she says.

She twists and turns on the couch. At last, thinking about Barney, who liked her and who is dead now, and George the school cat who gets fat on the cook's bacon ration, she falls asleep. She is woken by panting noises from the room next door. The panting gets more and more frantic – that awful man is hurting her mother! Laura leaps out of bed and rushes through the door into their room.

'Are you all right, Mummy?' She cannot remember when

she last called her mother *Mummy*.

'Yes, yes, go back to bed!'

'Shit!' Henry says.

So now Laura has a pretty clear idea of what *doing it* means: her mother with that man on top of her. She gets back into bed and holds her breath, listening for the panting to start again. How is she to get through the holidays listening out for that after ironing pieces of cloth all day?

She puts a pillow over her head.

She wakes not quite sure where she is. Sun is shining through the beige slightly torn curtains. She needs the bathroom but has forgotten where it is.

'Mummy…' she calls, but it is Henry who comes through the door.

'Had a good night's sleep, have you?'

'I've forgotten where the bathroom is,' she whispers.

'Speak up. I can't hear you!'

'I need the bathroom!' Laura yells at him.

He reminds her where it is.

She spends a good long time getting washed and dressed.

'Breakfast is served, your ladyship!' Henry shouts. He is in a buoyant mood.

The three of them sit down at the table, Ruth in a thin dressing gown, which falls open to reveal her breasts.

Laura looks away.

'Coming to the flicks with us tonight?' Henry asks.

When Laura's face does not light up, he adds, 'My treat.'

Laura's face still does not light up.

They chew their way through half burnt toast with marge and a scrape of some red jam.

'We should get Marmite again,' Laura says.

'He doesn't like Marmite.'

Henry wipes his mouth with the back of his hand and

gets up. 'I'm off!'

'Vair?' Ruth asks anxiously.

'To see a man about a dog!'

'But it's Saturday!'

'Yes, all day,' Henry bends down and kisses Ruth smackingly on the mouth. Then he turns to Laura.

'Want a kiss?'

Laura does not know where to look.

He disappears.

As soon as he has gone, Ruth asks, 'Vy you don't like him?'

'Was he hurting you in the night?' Laura asks.

'Of course not. Ve go shopping now?'

The butcher gives Ruth a small piece of rump steak from under the counter. 'For your little man!'

Laura hates the way the butcher grins at her mother. 'I'm off to the library!' she says. She remembers where it is from when Ruth lived in Golders Green before.

'Vy not come back viz me? I don't sink Henry vill be back before evening.'

Laura shakes her head.

She signs up at the library and takes out one of Mazo de la Roche's *Whiteoaks Chronicles* – not exactly revision work but something she's already found in the school library. It gives her the same kind of woozy sensations as Mrs. Wilson's American film magazines. She finds a bench in Golders Hill Park and starts reading. She has no idea how long she has been sitting on the bench when someone says,

'It's our little Laura, isn't it?'

She looks up and there is Hannah Karlsberg smiling at her. She is so pleased she jumps up and kisses her. Hannah strokes her cheek. Then Klaus, with another man and woman, catches up. They invite Laura to walk with them.

'We're staying with my brother-in-law, quite near here,'

Hannah says and then goes on, 'I thought you went to the country with the Quaker ladies for the summer holidays?'

For a moment Laura says nothing. She is so happy to be with Hannah, someone who really likes her. And then it all comes pouring out: not being wanted in Somerset, having to have a job ironing, her mother living with Henry.

Hannah strokes her cheek again. 'Would you like me to talk to your mother?'

'Would you really? Now? It's not far from here; I don't think Henry will be there!'

When Ruth sees Hannah on the doorstep, she changes almost instantaneously into the person she used to be in Berlin. Hannah asks if perhaps it might do if Laura worked mornings only; she is welcome to spend the afternoons with them. They are in London for most of the summer; Klaus is taking a refresher course at the London Hospital – he has to pass his exams in English.

'Vy not?' Ruth agrees. 'Ze boss at ze vorkshop von't mind, he only does it as a favour to me, anyvay.'

Laura looks at Hannah. She is bursting with gratitude.

On Monday morning Ruth takes Laura along to the textile workshop. A grey-haired man looks her up and down.

'So this is the young lady! Well, I could have taken you for her sister, not her mother,' he says, patting Ruth on the shoulder.

When Ruth has left, he says, 'You only want to work in the mornings? That's all right by me!'

Want! Laura thinks, but she says nothing as he takes her through to a large room where two women are ironing and the wireless is blaring out *Music While You Work*.

One of them says, ''Allo there, dearie, 'ere you are, 'ave this one then,' and she makes room for Laura at her ironing board while she sets up another one for herself. 'And mind, don't let the iron get too 'ot!'

'I'm only here mornings,' Laura tells them almost at once.

'Oo's a lucky girl, then,' the other woman says and then both of them sing along to the music *Mareseadoatsandozyeadoatsandlittlelambseativy...*'

Laura stands at the board in a dream, ironing piece after piece of fabric. She likes the smell of the warm ironed stuff. What will she tell the others at school about her summer holidays? She will censor this ironing episode, and Henry and those panting noises; you don't mention that kind of thing about your mother! She comes to when there is a sudden silence – the wireless is switched off.

'One o'clock, dearie,' one of the women says, 'I'm 'avin a cuppa at the ABC, want to come?'

'I'm going to have lunch with a friend,' Laura says and she feels the word *lunch* clunk heavily to the ground.

'Okydoky,' the woman says, but her face has gone stiff and she turns away.

It takes Laura twenty minutes to walk to where Hannah is staying. She passes a flower-shop with snapdragons in a bucket standing outside and spends sixpence of the shilling for bus fares Ruth gave her on a bunch for Hannah. She picks off one of the pink blossoms so she can snap it. Good word *snapdragon.*

'You shouldn't,' Hannah says when Laura gives her the flowers, but her face lights up.

After lunch, which is macaroni with a bit of grated cheese on top, they go to the park. They find a bench near the animal enclosures where a notice says *Please do not feed the animals,* but there are no animals.

'Gone for the duration,' Hannah says.

They scatter breadcrumbs for the starlings, blackbirds, a thrush and a few pigeons.

'Starlings look sort of prehistoric, don't they?' Laura says.

'Do they? Well, perhaps…' Hannah looks at her oddly.

Laura wonders if she has said something peculiar.

'Did you find the ironing very exhausting?' Hannah asks her. 'I hate ironing!'

They laugh as they walk out of the park along Golders Green Road. Hannah sighs.

'What shall I give Klaus for supper?'

Laura feels that question to be a kind of dismissal.

'I'd better go back now.' She doesn't say *home*.

'Will your mother be there?'

'I've got the key,' and then, very shyly, 'May I come again tomorrow after work?'

'Of course you may!'

'Can I bring my book of Tennyson poems? I got it as a literature prize!'

'Well done! Of course, bring it. I don't know much English poetry; you'll have to teach me!'

Laura dawdles after she has left Hannah. She passes the flower shop again but does not spend the other sixpence on a bunch for her mother.

When she gets to the house, there is a letter addressed to Ruth on the hall table. Laura recognises Aunt Ann's writing. Ruth is not back yet and Laura sits staring out of the window, looking at the front gardens opposite with their geometrical beds of standard roses, fuchsias, hydrangeas – town flowers. She misses the Meadow House garden where nothing is neat but everything seems to come up in the right place: snowdrops, daffodils, lavender, sweet scented stock, phlox, lupins, tiny pink roses in clusters, yellow poppies and, later, autumn crocuses, Michaelmas daisies, asters, small bronze chrysanthemums…

She lays the table. There is a blue and white checked table-cloth with one or two small holes in it, but she cannot find napkins. The plates in the kitchen do not match, and some are chipped. Maybe soon they will have their own things from Berlin that are being stored in Somerset?

Ruth gets in, looking tired. She lights a cigarette and takes her shoes off. Laura gives her the letter from Aunt Ann. As soon as she has read it, Ruth scrumples it up.

'Vot a bitch! Ve have to vait for our sings! Vy? It's our property!'

Laura smoothes out the scrumpled letter. It says that the cost of sending all those wooden crates would be prohibitive and probably impossible with the present transport restrictions for civilians. Best to wait til the war is over.

After a while Laura asks, 'Where would we put everything?'

'Zat's not ze question! You sink zey vant to keep our sings?'

'No, of course not!'

'Next time you see zose old vimmen, you ask again, ze sings belong to you as vell!'

Laura knows she will do no such thing. Meadow House seems immeasurably remote but, as she turns the letter over, she notices there is a postscript: *We should be pleased to have Laura here for the last week of the summer holidays at the beginning of September.* Laura reads it out with great excitement.

'But you von't vant to go?'

'Yes, I do, very much!'

'So, you don't like it viz your muzzer?'

Laura says nothing. She does so wish she *did* like it with her mother.

'Sank you for laying ze table,' Ruth says. 'Vot did Hannah

talk about? Very clever, alvays top of ze class at school, not like me, but she vasn't good at gym, I beat her zair!'

Henry comes in wearing his oily overalls. He kisses Ruth and then makes straight for the bathroom.

'I'll have my five inch bath,' he says with a grin.

Laura knows he will take more water than is allowed.

She gets paid ten shillings a week for doing the ironing. She offers the crackly brown note to Ruth; she knows her mother has to work hard for not much pay.

'You keep zis, you earned it,' Ruth says, but Henry tells her to accept it.

'Not necessary,' Ruth tells him.

There is the smoky tang of autumn in the garden when Laura gets to Meadow House. Rustling through the leaves she sees a black kitten.

'That's Tilly Kettle!' Aunt Ann says.

Laura picks the kitten up and kisses him. 'Him?' she asks.

'Yes, my lamb,' Aunt Edwina says.

'Let's see what the greengages are doing,' Aunt Ann says.

There is a ladder leaning against the tree. Aunt Ann climbs up it; she is quite old to be doing that. She drops the greengages into the trug Laura is holding with unerring aim, then climbs nimbly down. They wave to the gardener in his gaiters; he is stoking a bonfire.

'All well at home, Ben?' Aunt Ann calls.

'Yes, ma'am,' he calls back. 'We've got through the measles and Jack loved the books you sent!'

'And your chest?'

'Can't complain,' Ben says. His words come out with soft burring sounds.

Nice, Laura thinks, *different kind of English again.*

'He never does complain,' Aunt Ann says to Laura, 'but

he's had quite a bad time with his TB, which is why he's not been called up. He did complain about that!'

Aunt Ann's voice seems to have got gentler since Laura last saw her at school after Aunt Tessa died. She wants to say something like *It seems strange without Aunt Tessa here,* but she is too shy.

While Aunt Ann and Aunt Edwina are having their afternoon nap, Laura explores the bookshelves in the sitting room called the long parlour. There are a good many books about the local countryside, birds and wild flowers, and a whole shelf devoted to Quaker literature, the lives of George Fox and Elizabeth Fry, the history of Barclays bank and Huntley and Palmer biscuits and Clarks shoes, all started by Quakers. But it is to the slim volumes of poetry that Laura is drawn. There is one by someone called Emily Dickinson. It falls open at a short poem beginning:

> Hope is that thing with feathers
> That perches in the soul
> And sings the tune without the words
> And never stops at all.

Laura reads it out loud to herself. It's lovely though she is not sure what the tune of her hope is.

'Are you enjoying that?' Aunt Ann asks when she comes down from her rest.

Laura nods.

'Come and help make a tart with the greengages!'

She shows Laura how to rub margarine into the flour with her fingertips and add just a drop of water, gently, that'll do. Then she kneads and rolls it out so thinly that Laura thinks it is going to break, but it does not. They halve and stone the greengages, and Laura arranges them in overlapping lines on the pastry.

'No sugar', Aunt Ann says, 'but we'll use a spoonful of the WI honey.'

She gives Laura the spoon to lick.

Presently there is a delicious smell of baking pastry with honeyed fruit.

'Go and tell Aunt Edwina tea will be in the workroom.'

Laura runs upstairs to Aunt Edwina who is at her type-writer in a tiny study with a large window overlooking the garden.

'Coming, my lamb!'

The workroom is next door to the kitchen. They sit at a wooden table, six plain wooden chairs round it. The kitten jumps on Laura's knee and purrs loudly. Ben comes in.

'Done all there is to do for today,' he says.

'You'll have a cup of tea?'

He sits down opposite Laura. Aunt Edwina cuts a large slice of the greengage tart for him.

'Is the weather going to last?' she asks.

'Tomorrow and the day after, then we'll have rain.'

'Have we got enough logs?'

'Yes, plenty to keep going through the winter.'

Laura likes the way Ben says things as if he is quite certain of them. She also has the feeling that the three adults are saying more than the words, as if the words are only a cover for all sorts of meanings, good, safe meanings, making everything seem peaceful, even though there is a war on.

Later, they listen to the nine o'clock news. There have been massive bombing raids on Hamburg.

Good news, Laura thinks, *We're beating them!* Them?

Aunt Ann and Aunt Edwina shake their heads.

'All those civilians killed,' they murmur.

On the way up to bed Laura passes what was Aunt Tessa's room. The door is open; she puts her head round it and catches a whiff of mimosa scent. She wonders what really happens to people when they die. She can imagine another kind of world, a *somewhere else* where dead people go; different but still a bit the same, otherwise you couldn't even imagine it, just somewhere nothing nasty can ever happen to you again. She closes the door of Aunt Tessa's room. She would like that smell of mimosa to stay as long as possible.

In the room where she is sleeping there is a jug of shepherd's purse on the window sill – honesty. Aunt Ann has explained why it is called that. Laura crumbles one of the transparent, parchmenty envelopes and rubs the black seeds between her fingers. As she snuggles down in bed, she thinks about her grandpa who is dead, about her granny and her father, about whom there is no news. She can see them all so clearly inside herself. She shuts her eyes and takes a deep breath. Aunt Ann and Aunt Edwina do really seem to like her; and Hannah. Laura smiles as she remembers meeting her in Golders Hill Park. Is that the kind of thing God arranges? Then it occurs to her that perhaps round little Klaus gets on top of Hannah like Henry did on top of her mother. She wishes she had not thought of that.

She wakes to pale dawn light; it is very early, no one else is about. She gets dressed and tiptoes downstairs; she lets herself out by the backdoor through the kitchen. A few mauve autumn crocuses are showing in the long damp grass. She begins to run, past the field where they collect horse dung, past the greengage tree, past the spot where Barney is buried. She runs and runs, her heart hammering hard – *I'm here, I'm here, here!*

At school, there is an unusual seriousness about everyone in Laura's year as they realise School Certificate is only two and a half terms away. Laura is not the only one who wants her name on the honours board. But to her absolute dismay she *is* the only one who does not go down with German measles. One by one, all the others come out in the rash and are transferred to the sick rooms in the end house. Every morning Laura examines herself hopefully, but there is no sign of a rash.

'I suppose Germans don't catch German measles,' they say looking at her suspiciously.

It's no good trying to explain that in German, German measles are not called that. As far as she knows there is nothing specifically German about the disease and, *of course,* Germans catch it the same as anyone else.

'Then why haven't you?' they ask.

Never in her life has Laura so wanted to become ill.

Even Miss Elizabeth, when she is giving Laura extra Latin in the library on Saturday morning, looks at her with her head on one side. 'Lucky girl, not to go down with the German measles!'

When Laura starts to tell her, as she has told everyone else, that, in German, German measles are not called that, Miss Elizabeth pats her head and starts talking about gerunds.

When Laura goes to see Hannah and she welcomes her with the words, 'Good, you haven't got German measles; it's going round the whole town!' Laura bursts into tears. Over tea and a special treat of chocolate digestive biscuits, she tells Hannah and Klaus what the others have been saying.

'Surely you're not going to let such nonsense upset you?' They laugh.

Klaus pinches her cheek rather like her grandpa used to. She cheers up.

That afternoon instead of doing German, Hannah brings out a Halma board and shows Laura how to play. Concentrating on the game makes her forget everything else.

When she gets back to school, three of the girls, including Sheila, who have had German measles, are up and about again. 'Good old Laura!' they call out to her.

So they think she's all right, after all. How quickly the scene can change!

She has got into the First Hockey XI.

'Only because I'm so fat I fill the space between the goal posts!' The other ten laugh and pat her on the back. She is not really all that enormous, only not as skinny as most of the others. She just isn't an English shape,

They play matches against other schools on the sands. Laura enjoys buckling on the huge pads, enjoys kicking the ball right across the pitch – she has got good at that – and hardly uses her stick; so that when the centre forward of the opposing team breaks her stick after a cracking shot which misses the goal, Laura does not think twice about offering her stick to the girl. Afterwards, everyone crowds round Laura.

'Jolly decent of you to hand over your stick! And we won all the same!'

The referee, who teaches at the other school, comes up to Laura and shakes her hand. Odd to be made a fuss of for what felt like nothing much at all.

Sheila's mother comes to visit and invites Laura out tea.

'You'll come and stay with Sheila for a week or two, won't you? Maybe after the exams are over in the summer and you'll both have left Mentmore? You wouldn't mind helping with the beds and breakfast, would you? Sheila always does in the holidays. It's so hard to get staff with the war on!' Sheila's mother runs a small hotel in Devon.

Of course Laura would not mind. She had no idea Sheila liked her enough to invite her to stay.

The exams are held in a large hall near the town swimming baths. They have had it dinned into them to read the questions carefully twice over and to make their answers relevant. It's no good just pouring out everything you know. Laura does her best to remember that. After the exams are over, the art mistress takes them to an exhibition of the war artist Paul Nash. Most of the paintings and drawings are from the First World War, the one Laura's grandpa and father were in – on the other side, of course. But there is one painting called 'Dead Sea' of crashed aeroplanes which has been done quite recently. Laura stares and stares at it, overwhelmed by the silent devastation. They have extra art classes. Laura wishes she could transfer the sharp images she has onto the drawing paper, but there is something that just does not happen between her head and her hand. They also have history of art lessons with reproductions of old masters on a magic lantern. Laura specially loves Botticelli 'Primavera'. It strikes her as the very opposite of that daunting 'Dead Sea'.

On the last day of her last term at Mentmore, Laura takes herself down to the boot room and sobs in a dark corner. None of the other leavers is crying; they are excited about going home, about holidays, about what they are going to do next. Laura does not know what she is going to do next. Miss Elizabeth has tried to persuade her to stay on, to take Greek as well as Latin, to try for Oxbridge. She has even written to Ruth, who has sent back a curt, not to say rude, note, saying that Laura has to realise they are refugees; going to university is out of the question and besides, a daughter belongs with her mother in these difficult times.

'Laura, Laura, where are you?' Sheila is calling to her – they are going to Devon together.

'Coming!' Laura shouts back and makes herself stop crying. She fingers a letter from Aunt Ann in her pocket, wishing her well in her new life in London, hoping there will soon be news of her father and inviting her to Meadow House once she has settled into a new routine in London. There is a postscript from Aunt Edwina: *Keep us posted of your doings, my lamb!* They have taken it for granted that she will be living in London with her mother. Laura had hoped... that thing with feathers Emily Dickinson wrote about?

She hears footsteps coming down the stairs to the boot room. It is Miss Elizabeth herself.

'Laura, there you are, come along up, my dear, Sheila is waiting for you!'

She takes Laura gently by the hand and together they go back up into the hall where the staff are waiting to shake hands with the leavers. Miss Elizabeth walks down the drive with Laura.

'You must persuade your mother to find a school in London so that you can do your Higher School Certificate. Don't forget to write and tell us how you're getting on!'

Miss Elizabeth's bright blue eyes shine through her pince-nez.

Laura gets into the waiting taxi, peers out of the window, sees George, the school cat, snuffling round some catmint. The taxi turns out of the crescent. School is left behind.

'We'll have fun!' Sheila says in the train to Newton Abbot. 'Lots of boys!'

Laura feels a touch uncomfortable at the thought of boys. Sheila is a year older than she is; she has an older brother and is used to boys.

Her mother is at the station to meet them. She hugs Sheila and begins to cry. 'Now they're both missing!'

'Oh, God!' Sheila keeps her arms round her mother.

Laura does not know what to say. She knows Sheila's father and brother are both in the army in Singapore. She looks down at her feet waiting for the moment to pass.

'Good to be home,' Sheila says when they arrive at the small hotel.

They have grilled herrings for supper; Laura has never eaten such fresh fish. They sit in the kitchen in front of the Aga, which is like the one in Meadow House, sipping rough cider called scrumpy. *Good word,* Laura thinks.

'We'll have to hope and pray for the best,' Sheila's mother says, 'missing does not always mean dead. And in the meantime, we'll have to keep smiling, it's what they'd want.'

She pours herself some more cider.

'You girls have had enough. It's heady stuff this!'

Then she asks Laura how her mother is coping.

'Any news of your family?'

Laura says her grandpa is dead and that they don't know whether her granny in Theresienstadt or her father in Berlin are still alive.

After supper, they switch on the wireless for Tommy Handley's ITMA. For half an hour they laugh and laugh. *Can I do you now, sir – what do you want, we haven't got it!*

When they are in bed, Sheila asks, 'Do you think you'll go back home to Germany after the war? It's got to end some time, hasn't it?'

Laura is taken aback. England is home now, isn't it?

'I don't know,' she says. 'Depends what happens.' She does not add that they have not got a home in Germany now.

'Hope there's good news about your father and brother,' she says.

Sheila stretches out her hand and finds Laura's. They go to sleep holding hands.

At the weekend, Sheila's mother takes them to a Thé Dansant in a large hotel in Torquay.

'You girls have got to have your fun, war or no war!'

Laura puts on a red dress her mother got cheap from a refugee friend who has set himself up in the rag trade. She enjoys the feel of the slippery rayon against her skin. Sheila has given her a pair of nylons.

'A Yank left a whole lot of them after he stayed here!'

Laura fastens the stockings on her suspender belt. She hates wearing stockings, though her legs do look transformed by the nylons.

The band is playing Glen Miller's *Take the A Train* when they get to the hotel. They sit down at one of the little tables by the dance floor and almost immediately a naval cadet comes up to Sheila to ask her to dance. Laura watches them do the quickstep; Sheila dances well; Laura pretends she does not mind that no one has asked her. Sheila's mother is chatting to the woman at the next table. When the MC announces the Conga, she gets up, takes Laura by the hand.

'Come on, we can all do this!'

Sheila has not stopped dancing, though now she is with a different naval cadet – there is a group of them smoking by the window. Somebody grabs hold of Laura's waist and off they go in a long line – *ayayayayayay conga*. She can do this. Her hair flies about; there is not much perm left in it; she is quite sorry when the music stops. The person behind her has swivelled her round to face him. He has bright blue eyes and floppy fair hair. The MC announces a polka. Laura has learnt how to do that in dancing classes at school.

'Come on, let's have a go,' the young man says. 'I'm Bob!'

'Laura,' she says. It could be, it *is*, an English name.

They go stomping round the room. Then, suddenly, the lights are dimmed, there is total silence, everyone stands stiffly to attention as the band strikes up *God Save The King*. Then there is a renewed hum and buzz of conversation as people prepare to leave.

Bob takes Laura back to her table. It turns out that Sheila's mother and her friend know him and his family. *How nice,* Laura thinks, *they all know each other.*

'My dad's home on leave!' Bob says.

Laura can see the pain in Sheila's mother's face.

'Another three days before he goes back to his squadron,' Bob tells them. 'He's a bit browned off because they haven't seen any action yet!'

Sheila's mother introduces her to her friend, saying her full name.

'That sounds foreign,' the friend says, as if she has smelt a bad smell.

Sheila's mother explains. How Laura wishes she did not have to go through that rigmarole every time people hear her German name: refugee… mother Jewish… grandparents deported… father stayed behind…not Jewish…not a Nazi, of course…

'I see,' the friend says, still smelling the bad smell, and goes on, 'As far as I'm concerned, the only good German's a dead German!' She smiles patriotically.

Laura looks at Bob. He does not seem fazed by the revelation that her second name is a German one.

'I have to get back to the pigs,' he says – he is at the local agricultural college. 'Come to the flicks with me at the weekend? It's *For Whom the Bell Tolls,* with Ingrid Bergman.'

So it really doesn't matter about her name. Bob likes her!

Sheila has gone off with one of the naval cadets. Laura waits while Sheila's mother says goodbye to her friend.

'What a pity Sheila didn't bring a little English girl to stay,' she says without lowering her voice.

Sheila's mother hooks her arm through Laura's as they walk to the station, past a poster telling them that *Careless talk costs lives.*

It is Laura's last day in Newton Abbot, she is waiting for Bob to call for her.

'I bet he takes you into the double seats in the back row!' Sheila says. 'So you won't see much of the picture!'

'I'm looking forward to the film,' Laura says innocently. 'It's based on a novel by Ernest Hemingway. I'll get it out of the library when I get back home – I mean, back to London.'

Ruth has moved again, from Golders Green to West Hampstead. Laura has no idea where the nearest library is.

Sheila looks at her blankly. 'You've never been kissed, have you?' she asks.

Laura looks at her feet, embarrassed. Her school shoes do not really go with the tight-waisted cotton frock she is wearing.

Yes, Bob has tickets for the double seats. He puts his arm round her and his slightly stubbly cheek near hers. It feels nice, but she forgets about it when the film starts. Presently, his arm slips from her shoulder to her waist; he pulls her towards himself and kisses her. There is a whiff of hay about him. That's nice too, but Laura wishes he would wait until the film is over – it is really gripping. When his hand slips from her waist to her breast and he puts his tongue in her mouth, she closes her eyes.

The lights come on. *God Save the King* starts. They stand up.

'Did you enjoy the picture?' Sheila's mother asks when they get back.

They nod. Bob asks Laura how much longer she is staying.

'Back to London tomorrow!'

'I'll write!'

Now, *now*, Laura would like him to kiss her, but he does not. She walks with him to the end of the drive, where he has left his bicycle.

'I'll get your address from Sheila,' he says and pedals away, turning round once to wave, making the bike wobble.

'I don't like to think of you in London with those dreadful doodlebugs going off all the time!' Sheila's mother says as she is seeing Laura off at Newton Abbot station.

'Oh, I'll be all right!'

'Course you will,' Sheila says.

The train pulls out. Laura wonders how she knows she will be all right.

§

'Here ve are,' her mother says as they get to the attic flat in West Hampstead. She flings the sitting room door open with a flourish and, there, set out on a rickety table, Laura sees crystal glasses sparkling green, blue, crimson, purple, apricot. The last time she saw those they were in a glass-fronted cabinet in her grandparents' Berlin flat. So, their things *have* come from Somerset.

'Vell?' Ruth smiles at Laura. 'Now vot you say?'

Laura would like to say that they need a room to go with the glasses. She looks at the frayed curtain sliding off its rail, the sagging armchairs, the grimy walls. She sees crates upturned on top of each other to make a sort of dresser. In them are fluted china coffee cups with a pattern of black and yellow flowers and piles of damask tablecloths with matching napkins done up in blue satin ribbons. There is silver cutlery including fish knives and forks with sea creatures embossed on them. And there, too, yes, *yes*, is a little glass cage with two yellow glass birds in it.

'That's mine!'

Her granny gave her that when birthdays were real. *Two*

goldfinches for my little goldfinch.

'Where's my room?' Laura asks.

The room is tiny with sloping walls. *This is my room? This is who I am?* Laura asks herself.

'You unpack,' Ruth says. 'I make supper.'

Laura puts the glass cage on the table standing against the wall. She gets out the raffia chimney sweep and stands him next to the goldfinch cage. She hangs her clothes in the wardrobe which takes up too much space, stacks her books on the table – there are too many. Maybe there is a bookshelf in the other room? Laura remembers there was a crate of books; her father made sure of that. She goes into the kitchen to ask Ruth about it.

'Oh zat, ve left it behind, zose books vould have been too much.'

Books too much? But not crystal glasses? Not fish knives and damask tablecloths? Laura looks at Ruth. *This is my mother?*

She writes to thank Sheila's mother, called a *bread-and-butter letter* – Aunt Edwina told her that. She wonders, but does not ask, if Bob has got her address.

'Ze day after tomorrow ve have ze appointment at Bloomsbury House,' Ruth says over supper.

'What's Bloomsbury House?'

'A charity for Jewish refugees.'

So that label, which had begun to fade, still clings to her.

She feels acutely uncomfortable on the way to see someone who hands out second-hand clothes. After a good deal of rummaging about, the woman fishes out a camel hair coat.

'This should fit!'

Laura tries it on – yes, it fits. She looks at herself in the full length mirror on the wall. It does not look too bad, but as she takes it off, she sees a huge pale stain, a gray mess, on the back of it.

'I can't wear this!'

'Oh well,' the woman's voice is icy, 'someone will.'

'Ve take it,' Ruth says quickly. 'Sank you.'

Laura thinks she would rather freeze to death than put that coat on ever again.

'Ze stain doesn't show so much.' Ruth says when they are out of the room.

'Not if you're blind.'

Ruth changes the subject. 'Now ve see someone about a school for you.' She had found a job for Laura in the office of the place where she had done the ironing; they would have paid for shorthand and typing courses, but after some tense discussions Ruth finally agreed that Laura should go back to school for two more years.

The woman concerned with schools suggests one on the Highgate side of Hampstead Heath. 'Wonderful headmistress, has the greatest sympathy with and understanding for Jewish refugees, a good many in the school.'

No getting away from that, Laura thinks. Is she turning into a refugee from being a refugee?

Ruth smiles and nods approvingly.

The woman makes an appointment with the headmistress's secretary.

'Then you'll be fixed up for the beginning of the autumn term,' she smiles at Laura.

Whatever the school turns out to be like, Laura feels relieved to have an autumn term in prospect.

Meeting the new headmistress, who has a kind of other-worldly look about her, goes well. She asks Laura what subjects she would like to take.

'English and French,' she says immediately. Then she hesitates, but almost against her will she adds, 'And German...'

her grandfather's *Don't forget your mother tongue* echoing inside her.

She gets her School Certificate results from Miss Elizabeth. Yes, she has Matric Exempt. *Well done! You'll have to come and see your name up on the honours board,* Miss Elizabeth writes.

'I've done it, I've done it!' Laura shouts waving the letter in her mother's face.

'I'm proud of my clever daughter,' Ruth says and hugs her. 'Ve go to a Vill Hay show at ze Golders Green Hippodrome to celebrate,' she promises. Someone at the munitions factory knows Will Hay and gives Ruth free tickets. Laura has no idea who Will Hay is. She wonders how the others at Mentmore have done, writes to Sheila, asks if Bob ever got her address, then scrumples the letter up and starts again. She writes to tell Aunt Ann and Aunt Edwina, to Klaus and Hannah – they will all be pleased.

Then she looks at the awful coat from Bloomsbury House hanging in the wardrobe and vows never to wear it; she will earn money to buy a coat of which she is not ashamed. So she spends the rest of the summer holiday back ironing pieces of fabric. When Ruth says she does not have to, Laura tells her mother she wants decent clothes. She also spends some of her earnings on whitewash for her room. There are congratulations from Hannah, enclosing a postal order for five shillings, but there is nothing from Meadow House. Laura is sad about that. Tilly Kettle will no longer be a kitten.

On the first day of the autumn term, Laura is wearing new clothes bought with her own money. Her coat from Bloomsbury House is in the dustbin. You don't have to wear uniform in the sixth form.

'You're new, aren't you? For the Lower Sixth?' a member

of staff says as Laura walks into the red brick school building. She is the only new girl in the class; the other nine have all been there since they were eleven. The headmistress comes to talk to them. She tells them that being sixth formers is pretty well like being university students; they will no longer be spoon fed but be expected to use their own initiative in all sorts of ways. Then she introduces Laura to the others. Two of them have continental sounding names but, like Laura, they speak English without the least trace of a foreign accent. Another girl is English Jewish – being Jewish in London is not as strange as it was in Weston-super-Mare.

They sit at a long table, not desks, waiting for the English mistress. She turns out to be rather large with fine fair hair done up in a tight knot.

'Hallo everyone! Had a good summer? Nice to see you all. We're kicking off with Spenser; I'll tell you a bit about him, then we'll take it in turns to read. I see your edition has asterisks every now and then. Tell me when you come to them and I'll fill you in!' That does make them feel like university students.

After the mid-morning break, they have more English with a different teacher who is reading Shaw's *St. Joan* with them. Heidi, one of the other refugee girls, is given the part of St. Joan; Laura gets the part of Dunois. They enjoy the play reading. At the end of the school day Laura and Heidi catch the train from Gospel Oak to West Hampstead together.

When Laura gets back to the flat, there is a nasty smell from the kitchen. She finds stinking fish and turned milk; there is no refrigerator – not many people have one. She pours the sour milk down the sink, wraps the fish in newspaper and takes it down to the dustbins. She is hungry – it seems a long time since she had her marmite sandwiches and an apple for lunch. Nearly everyone brought sandwiches – quite a change of scene from going into lunch at Mentmore with Miss Thomas saying grace and then, if you were sitting at her table, talking French with Mademoiselle, everyone hoping someone would pass them the gravy or the salt, not being allowed to ask for it yourself.

Now she finds some stale but not inedible bread and makes tea in the brown pot. She remembers the smoky smell of Lapsang Souchong at Meadow House in cups bordered with red and purple flowers; remembers pale amber tea in glasses in silver holders that her granny put on a small white china tray. She takes the tea into her room, which is bright with the recent whitewash, gets *St. Joan* out of her schoolbag and immerses herself in Shaw's take on this quasi-mythical girl. On the whole, people who hear voices are considered mad; but Laura can hear her father's and grandparents' voices quite clearly inside herself.

Ruth comes in looking pale and tired and spends a long time in the bathroom cleaning up. Her nails are broken, the pink nail polish chipped.

'Zey give us gloves but I can't do ze vork viz gloves,' she says, rubbing cream into her hands. 'How can I give people a massage viz hands like zese!' She holds them up. 'All zat training at home vasted!'

At home: Berlin.

Laura mentions the fish.

'Vot? You srew it avay?'

'It stank!'

'Vell zen, ve can't eat it!' Ruth bursts out laughing.

They have fried potatoes and pickled beetroot out of a jar for supper.

Laura falls into the new routine: quick breakfast with her mother, train to school – she is making friends, getting quite good marks for essays – then back to the flat to do homework. Mentmore days are receding, though Sheila keeps in touch. She has not gone back to any school, is helping her mother with the hotel work and enjoying herself with Dartmouth naval cadets. There is still no definite news about her father and brother. She does not mention Bob.

Always when her mother comes home, Laura feels a little jolt of pleasure, but after the first five minutes there is nothing to talk about. She has no idea what went on in Ruth's day at the factory; Ruth has no idea what Spenser and Shaw are about. Anything she can think of saying immediately strikes Laura as pointless. She hates it when Ruth asks if she is feeling all right. Sometimes she fantasizes about having an English mother without forming any distinct image of what such a mother might look like. An English mother would probably have been brought up in the country, part of a large family. It would be fun to have English aunts and uncles and cousins. An English mother might be widowed, certainly not divorced. She does not fantasize about having an English father: she loves her real father. Sometimes she sits in her room by candlelight reading Keats or First World War poems.

The Second World War goes on around her. Doodlebugs have been superseded by the even deadlier V2s.

'Vot's ze point of going to a shelter viz zose sings,' Ruth says when the air raid warning goes. Quite often the rocket has already landed, so far always somewhere else. Every now and then she looks at Laura and says, *'Schrecklich, schrecklich!'* She picks up the raffia chimney sweep, 'You still have zis!'

There is no news from Germany. They have not had a letter from their friends in Switzerland for a long time. One morning, when she has stopped expecting it, Laura has a letter from Aunt Ann: Aunt Edwina has died; she is selling

Meadow House; it is too lonely without her friends. She is moving into a Quaker retirement home where they welcome pets, so she can take Tilly Kettle, who is quite a sedate cat now. *A great comfort,* she says and *Be sure to let me know if there is news from your father.* And she adds congratulations about getting the Matric Exempt.

Laura reads the letter three times. When she shows it to Ruth, Ruth shrugs her shoulders and says, 'You write. I von't.'

Laura does not know what to say. She has never had to write a letter of condolence. When that red card from Theresienstadt signed *Widow* arrived, there was no way of replying. She sucks her pen, remembers how Aunt Edwina called her *my lamb.*

Getting on the train in West Hampstead every morning, Laura notices a boy who goes to the school next door to hers. They have not spoken, but he has smiled in her direction. Then one day he moves over to sit next to her.

'I'm Johnny,' he says.

'Laura.'

They walk the short distance to school together; every now and then his sleeve rubs against hers. Laura likes the way he strides along as if the world belongs to him. After school, there he is, standing on the platform.

'You waited for me?' Laura feels herself blushing.

He nods. 'You're new this year, aren't you?'

She tells him about the boarding school she used to go to. 'But being a day girl is much better,' she says. *Is it?*

Johnny gets off the train with her. 'I'll walk you home!'

Laura is not quite comfortable with that. Will he expect her to ask him in? She does not want him to see their dilapidated attic flat with the makeshift packing-case dresser full of things from what seems like a previous incarnation. Ruth has been selling the crystal glasses for a pound each; Laura does not know whether or not that is a good price for them.

'See you tomorrow,' is all Johnny says when they get to her house, and he smiles. That smile gets to her.

He sees her home most days. He tells her how he wants to be a journalist in Paris. Yes, he is good at French, has a French grandfather. Laura almost tells him her father is a German journalist but stops herself – it would need too much explaining.

'Paris when the Jerries have finally been turfed out... won't be long now!' Johnny says.

Laura is very glad she has not let on that she is a sort of Jerry.

One afternoon, Johnny does not say *See you tomorrow* as they get to Laura's house. He says, 'It's about time I kissed you!'

They stand in the dusk in her doorway. His face, his very beautiful face, comes closer and closer; she inclines her head towards his, too breathless to speak. He kisses her, presses his whole body against hers.

Then he says, 'You haven't done much of this, have you?'

Laura does not know where to look.

'Never mind; you will!' Johnny says and walks away.

They do not coincide on the train again.

The Lower Sixth go as a group to the Christmas dance at the boys' school next door. Laura is reluctant to go. Johnny has made her lose confidence, but he does not seem to be at the dance, and to her surprise a dark-haired boy comes up to her almost at once. They do a quickstep without talking. The boy dances rather well; Laura finds it easy to follow him. He gets her a glass of orange squash.

'I'm Jewish, you know. My parents came as refugees from

Berlin,' he says before even telling her his name.

Why is that the first thing he mentions? In case she does not want to talk to him because he is Jewish? Has that happened to him?

'That's where I come from, too,' Laura says without adding she is only half Jewish. *Only?*

'That's OK then. I'm Fred,' he smiles at her.

'Laura,' she says, though on this occasion it would be all right to add her second name without embarrassment.

He invites her to his house, introduces her to his parents. They have been in England much longer than Laura and her mother and live in style with furniture they brought out from Berlin. *Why didn't we?* Laura wonders. Fred is an enthusiastic cyclist; he has a speedometer on his Rudge racing bike. When Laura confesses she cannot ride a bike, he laughs and offers to teach her. It does not take her long to learn.

He lends her one of his three bikes and they go for long rides in the countryside round London. On one occasion in the spring they go to Milton's cottage in Chalfont St. Giles; Laura has Miss Elizabeth's voice echoing inside her, reading the sonnet 'On His Blindness'. They picnic in woods and fields, the English countryside gentle round them. Sheltered by trees, they stretch out on last year's leaves and Fred tells Laura how pretty she is; this makes her want him to kiss her before he actually does. They forget about being refugees.

When she goes away for a week to stay with Sheila in Devon, Fred writes to her; Sheila is impressed. There is a muted atmosphere about the little hotel – Sheila's father and brother have both been confirmed dead. What to say? Laura hugs Sheila and her mother. Just before she leaves, Bob turns up. How nice he looks in his cords and tweed jacket! There is something mercurial about him that moves Laura deeply, something rather like the weather, one minute grey, the next silver and turquoise. Is it his Englishness? He says nothing about not having got in touch but makes her feel they are friends. When, after he has left, Sheila tells her he has a new girlfriend, it makes no difference to that feeling.

Back in London, it is too wet and windy to go for long bike rides with Fred. Instead, he gets her to come to his parents' flat when they are out. Sitting on the sofa, he fondles her in new and delightful ways. They lose track of time but then, afterwards, drinking fizzy orange straight out of the Corona bottle, they do not have a great deal to say to each other. Fred is going straight into his father's furniture business when he leaves school. When Laura says she wants to get a degree, he asks 'What for?' She does not know what to answer, but she would rather be with someone who did not ask her that. She sees less of Fred.

Laura's last year at school begins. Everyone else is getting geared up for college. She has talked to her mother about going to university, tells her she could get a grant.

'You forget ve are refugees,' is all she hears from Ruth.

'Some of the others are as well!'

'Vell, perhaps zey have fahzers viz a lot of money! Ven you leave school, you get a job! Is zat understood?'

In November the Sixth Form girls are encouraged to sign up as temporary postmen for the Christmas holidays to help deliver cards. Just before the end of term they are called for interview to the GPO in Mount Pleasant. The hall is crowded; names are called; Laura sits up expectantly, but the man calling out names does not call hers. Heidi is also still sitting there when everyone else has been called. The man comes up to them, asks who they are, passes a finger down a long list, shakes his head, looks a bit surprised, says, 'Sorry, enemy aliens not allowed!' *So that's what I've turned into,* Laura thinks.

Feeling gutted, she walks out into the cold with Heidi.

Laura concentrates on her work. She may not be going to college but she wants to get the best grades she can.

The six of them doing English go to the New Theatre in St. Martin's Lane to see the Old Vic Company doing *King Lear*. They get there at six in the morning to queue for stools; they listen to the buskers – one banging spoons on his knees is always there. Then they queue again in the evening for the one and sixpenny tickets up in the gallery. Laura goes to see *King Lear* three times, not only because it is a set book but because Laurence Olivier as Lear and Alec Guinness as the Fool open up new dimensions of tragedy for her, making it both personal and universal.

She goes to see French films at the Academy and Studio One in Oxford Street to get her ear in and her accent improved for the oral exam. She does not need to practise her German accent; what she enjoys most about the German course is Rilke's poetry – the way he uses the German language surprises and delights her.

The war is coming to a frightening end. In February 1945, Dresden is destroyed by two incendiary raids in one night. In April, Belsen concentration camp is liberated; what newsreels and papers reveal sends shockwaves through the nation. *These almost-corpses are people I might have known?* Laura thinks. On May 8th, European victory is celebrated. Ruth and Laura listen to the King's broadcast:

War battered but never for one moment daunted or dismayed… Our cause was the cause not of the nation only, not of this Empire and Commonwealth only, but of every land where freedom is cherished and law and liberty go hand in hand.

They hear Churchill:

My dear friends, this is your hour!… I say that in the long years to come not only will the people of this island but of the world, where the bird of freedom chirps in human hearts, look back to what we have done... Now we have emerged from one deadly struggle – a terrible foe has been cast on the ground and awaits our judgment and our mercy.

But in July Churchill is defeated by Clement Attlee in the General Election. There has not been a Labour Government since 1931. Laura is not quite sure of the significance of all this; could we have won the war without Churchill? But she does understand that men who have fought side by side will no longer put up with touching their caps and being called *My good man* by some toff in brogues.

There is still no news of her father or her granny or any of the other relations who left Berlin in one way or another. Bernard, one of Ruth's young cousins, was sent out to Bangkok to make his way with Unilever; every now and then she mentions him hopefully.

As soon as the exams are over, Laura goes for job interviews with publishing firms; she feels comfortable in the world of books and print. At the first interview, it turns out they wanted someone older. At the second, the woman interviewing fiddles with the cross round her neck and tells her that, though in many ways she seems the right sort of girl for the job, they could not possibly employ someone with a German surname like hers; what would the liftman say, who's just lost a leg in the war? At the third interview, the man who sees her treats her at once as if she were a fellow member of staff and does not comment on her foreign-sounding name. He explains that theirs is a strict union house and that she will automatically belong to the clerical union. He adds regretfully that, if he allowed her to write so much as a caption for a photograph, he would be in deep trouble with *his* union. Laura takes the job, puts herself down for shorthand and typing classes and looks forward to a youth-hostelling holiday before she begins life as an office girl.

'You sink ve vill hear from your fahzer now?' Ruth asks as she sees Laura off on her bike.

It is not comfortable to have a mother who says *your fahzer* like that, as if he had no connection with her.

'And granny?' Laura looks at her mother.

Ruth looks away.

Laura meets Heidi who has got into Bedford College to do English. Heidi has come with her brother, who has brought a friend. While they cycle across the countryside towards Stratford-on-Avon, the Japanese capitulate. Atom bombs have been dropped on Hiroshima and Nagasaki. The horrifying photographs of bomb victims in the papers dampen the spirit of relief and jubilation.

In Stratford they go to see *The Tempest*. Once the curtain has gone up, Laura forgets everything, until Prospero breaks his magic staff. She is sitting next to Heidi's brother's friend. He has been scribbling in a notebook, only looking up occasionally through horn-rimmed spectacles to take in what is happening on the stage. While they are clapping, Laura asks him what he has been writing. Alec holds the notebook open and she sees he has been sketching the characters on the stage. On the way back to the youth hostel he tells her he has got into Camberwell School of Art.

'And what about you?' he asks.

'Publisher's office in Long Acre,' she mumbles.

'That's near the opera house, isn't it?'

'Right opposite!'

'We'll go,' he promises. He does not seem put off by the fact that she is not going to college.

She gets back to West Hampstead in good spirits, but the moment she looks at Ruth's face, everything she was going to tell her mother about the holiday dries up inside her.

'Sit down, dahlink... ve have to talk... I have to tell you...' but Ruth gets no further. She sobs and sobs. Laura holds her hand.

'Zis voman came vile you vere avay, told me everysink, how in ze end...'

How in the end Laura's granny was in one of the last batches – *batches?* – who were gassed in Auschwitz.

'Zis voman, much younger, could still vork, zat's how she survived... said zat... zat after grandpa died granny vent out of her mind... how she looked after her like a daughter... but... but... *I* am ze daughter!'

Laura goes on holding her mother's hand. People's grannies die all the time, don't they; it's what you expect grannies to do... only... only... not... not... How can she talk about *The Tempest*, about Prospero and his magic staff? In spite of the awful news, Laura somehow feels her lovely granny safe inside her. Nothing can stop her from being her granny's little goldfinch.

There is a letter from Aunt Ann. Ruth gives it to Laura.

'Perhaps she has heard from your fahzer?'

But Aunt Ann is only writing to ask if *they* have had any news. She goes on to say that she has settled quite comfortably into the retirement home, and so has Tilly Kettle. Tilly Kettle! Laura can feel his fur soft and warm under her hands. She starts to cry and will not let Ruth put an arm round her. She runs into her room.

Before she has got round to replying to Aunt Ann, there is a letter, readdressed many times, from their Swiss friends. Inside the envelope, there is another envelope with a letter from one of her father's colleagues. *How sad I am,* it says in German, *to have to tell you that your father perished in a bomb attack over Berlin on...* Laura reads no further, drops the letter on the floor.

'Vot you doing?' Ruth picks it up, reads it, puts a hand on Laura's shoulder. Laura pulls away.

'I don't understand you!' Ruth says.

Nothing to understand, Laura thinks. Like her granny and grandpa, her father is safe inside her, but she cannot explain that to her mother.

§

The publisher who appointed Laura introduces her to his colleagues. One of them raises his eyebrows when he hears her name. 'Sounds suspiciously German,' he says and walks off.

Suspiciously? Isn't the war over?

Everyone else shakes her warmly by the hand. One of the secretaries shows her how to do filing, takes her out to lunch and asks if she is doing shorthand and typing classes. Laura goes to them reluctantly. They type to music on typewriters with covered keyboards; everyone giggles; they make a lot of mistakes. She decides not to bother with touch typing; she is managing reasonably well on the large Remington on her desk in the office. Shorthand is more interesting – she passes the first test easily. Not long after she has had the news about her father, her boss asks if she can manage to take a letter in shorthand. She can, but she has to start the typing three times because she does not want to use the rubber, which will make holes in the austerity-quality paper. When she finally takes the letter to be signed, her boss says, 'Well done!' and pats her on the knee. Laura almost tells him about her father but just then his phone rings, so she goes away.

Ruth has stopped working at the munitions factory and has found a job as a masseuse with a beautician in the West End; an actor called Rufus whom she met at the Golders

Green Hippodrome has recommended her. Having done war work has made it easy for her to get the work permit.

Laura is usually first back in the flat, lights the smelly oil stove in her room, warms up some baked beans and eats them straight out of the tin. The raffia chimney sweep stands on her table; the broom has slipped out of his right hand, but he still has his ladder. She picks him up, shuts her eyes and feels her father's hand warm in hers as he gives her it on the Anhalter Bahnhof. Six years ago! She has an image of him in his short black overcoat with the velvet collar.

She writes to Aunt Ann in her retirement home, as well as to Hannah and Klaus who have moved to Yorkshire where Klaus has got a post as consultant anaesthetist – he passed all his exams in English – and before Ruth comes home, she goes to bed, looking forward to meeting Alec after work. Unlike Bob, he has kept in touch and they are going to see *La Bohème* in Covent Garden.

At breakfast, Ruth tells her that Rufus, the man who helped get her the job with the beautician, is coming to visit that evening.

'So you vill meet him!' Her voice carries instructions to be civil.

'I'll be out,' Laura says.

Ruth also shows her a letter from Henry, who has settled in Chicago near his sister. He has a new girlfriend but promises to help Ruth over if she wants to come, for old times sake.

'I knew he vould,' Ruth says.

Laura says nothing.

At the end of the office day, Laura walks out into the dusk; it is lovely to have the streets brightly lit after years of bumbling about with torches in the blackout. Rationing goes on; there are queues for bread and potatoes, and once she found herself in a queue which turned out to be for birdseed! Just as she was about to walk away, the woman behind her begged her to buy some – her canaries could do with a bit of extra!

Alec is waiting for her. He holds her hand as they cross the road to the opera house. Their seats are in the front row of the gallery, where there is adequate legroom. Puccini's music moves Laura to tears; perhaps she will tell Alec about her father. Afterwards, on the way to the underground, Alec tells her about life classes at Camberwell; about landscape drawing with Victor Pasmore; about learning to throw pots on the wheel; about a girl called Milly who is very good at that; about a fancy dress ball coming up just before Christmas – 1890s, Toulouse-Lautrec, that kind of thing; would she like to come? Of course! She has never been to a fancy dress ball. She does not let on that she is not quite sure who or what Toulouse-Lautrec is. She will find out. She does not mention her father.

'Margot Fonteyn's dancing in *Sleeping Beauty* tomorrow; I'll get up early to queue for tickets. And there's this amazing Van Gogh exhibition at the Tate – let's go Saturday morning!'

Laura is excited – opera, ballet, art, a fancy dress ball! Yes, yes, the war *is* over! As she unlocks the front door, she remembers that Ruth's friend Rufus might be there. The light is on in the front room but there is no one talking, instead there is the sound of sobbing. Laura opens the door gently to see Ruth curled up on the couch, head buried in a satin cushion, shoulders heaving. She turns a blotchy face towards Laura.

'It's all over,' she says crumpling a handkerchief in her hand.

Laura sees a bunch of yellow roses lying on the table. She picks them up – they need putting in water.

'Leave zem alone, srow zem avay!'

Laura drops the roses.

'*La Bohème* was lovely,' she says sheepishly. 'And ballet tomorrow night!'

Ruth sits up. Laura notices grey hair reappearing at her temples where the dye is fading. The black has an uncomfortable sheen of bronze about it.

'Tomorrow? You go out again tomorrow? If you...' Ruth sobs, 'go out tomorrow you vill find... I vill put my head in ze gas oven... if it's not enough for you to have your fahzer dead, your grandparents... zen you vill have a dead muzzer as vell!'

Laura cannot believe what she is hearing. Ruth looks across at the wilting roses.

'He came for five minutes to tell me zair is someone else, ze bastard!'

'You mean Rufus?' Laura asks stupidly. She is very tired.

'Don't ever say his name again!'

'Goodnight then!'

'Give your muzzer a kiss!'

Reluctantly Laura kisses her mother.

At breakfast Ruth says, 'So I see you here for supper. Vot vould you like to eat?'

'But...'

Ruth's chin trembles. 'If you vant to see me again alive you vill be here!'

Miserably, Laura goes to work. Miserably she meets Alec.

'I can't come out tonight, my mother isn't... isn't well.'

'Oh, it won't be hard to sell your ticket,' Alec says. 'See you at the Tate Saturday morning then?'

Laura wishes he sounded more disappointed. How lightly he walks away from her. Doesn't he mind at all? She knows that not showing you mind things is very English. She will try not to show it when *she* minds; but perhaps Alec *really* doesn't mind? How can you tell?

When she gets home, Ruth is standing in front of the bathroom mirror patting her face with a large pink powder puff; then she takes out a lipstick and paints her mouth crimson. She looks at Laura surprised.

'Back early? I sought you vere going out?'

'But...' Laura's heart is hammering hard.

'I go out in ten minutes,' Ruth says.

'With Rufus?' Laura asks bewildered.

'Don't be silly, of course not!'

The phone rings, Ruth rushes to answer it.

'Eddie, hallo, dahlink. I'm ready...'

Laura goes into her room, sits on her bed with clenched fists. She can hardly breathe; she has never been so angry in all her life. She looks at the raffia chimney sweep, at the little glass bird cage on her table. Gradually she calms down. In the morning, she eats her cornflakes in her room by herself.

She meets Alec on Saturday outside the Tate Gallery. The queue stretches right round the building; this is the first major exhibition since the war. After about two hours, they get in. Alec is almost trembling with excitement as they walk round – all he can say is, 'Look, look, look!' Laura looks. There are the sunflowers, the chair, the cornfield, the stars in the dark blue sky; there are the self portraits. Not picture postcards, the real thing! Alec is poring over glass cases with drawings.

'I'll have to come again!' he says, his grey eyes shining.

They stroll along Millbank, walk past the Houses of Parliament and down Whitehall into Trafalgar Square. Alec buys them hot meat pies and mugs of tea at a street stall. Laura is beginning to be a Londoner.

She gets ready for the 1890s fancy dress ball. She has made a pale blue high-necked taffeta blouse with a remnant she got without coupons. She goes looking for a long black skirt;

there is no time to make that as well – she has to pass another shorthand exam. So she swallows her pride and anger and asks Ruth, to whom she has been speaking as little as possible, if maybe her friend in the rag trade could…

'Of course, dahlink.' And a few days later Ruth produces a long black skirt for Laura, which does not look cheap.

'Thank you,' Laura mumbles.

'Do I get a kiss?'

No, Ruth does not get a kiss.

There is a crowd round the bar when Laura gets to Camberwell Art School. She cannot see Alec, but Heidi and her brother are there. He looks comic with a burnt cork moustache under his nose. Alec appears.

'Hallo, all!'

Laura is a bit hurt she is just one of the all.

'Here's Milly,' Alec says.

A young woman swathed in black velvet, her fair hair swept high on her head, steps out of the crowd. Laura looks at her face, *not such a very nice face,* she thinks. Perhaps faces don't matter so much if you're a wonderful shape?

Alec dances with Laura, but he keeps looking at other girls. 'There's a party at Milly's afterwards,' he tells her.

Laura, Heidi and her brother pile in to the back of Milly's old banger. Alec sits in the front next to her.

'A bit young, aren't they?' Laura hears Milly say as they go down some steps into her basement flat. How old is *she?* And Alec? Quite soon Milly's flat is jammed with couples on each other's knees, kissing in corners, shedding skirts, trousers. Laura cannot see Milly or Alec.

Heidi comes over to her. 'Shall we go?'

'You'll have to come to an IVC dance; they're really good,' Heidi says on their way home.

'IVC?'

'Intervarsity Vacation Club!'

'But I'm not a student!'

'Doesn't matter at all,' Heidi assures her.

The IVC dances are in Chelsea Town Hall along the King's Road. Laura sits waiting for someone to ask her to dance; she has almost forgotten why she is there.

'Will you have this dance with me?'

There is this young man with a long nose in his thin face looking at her, a mauve scarf flapping round his neck. He does not dance very well, but Laura likes the way he grips her firmly round the waist. Then he buys her a shandy at the bar. He is called Francis, has a degree in botany and works in a lab. 'But what I really do is write poetry,' he says.

Laura warms to him.

Suddenly he says, 'There's Tom!' in a voice loud enough to make everyone near them turn round, except this Tom, whoever he may be.

'Tom and I were at college together; he did zoology, but what he's brilliant at is philosophy. Couldn't do a degree in it because of the war, all philosophy departments closed down for the duration.' Francis speaks of this Tom with great admiration; Laura is not quite sure what being brilliant at philosophy involves.

Francis sees her to the bus stop along the King's Road and asks her to meet him in a coffee bar along Old Compton Street the following Saturday. 'Excellent coffee there!' he says. Laura dare not tell him she does not like coffee. Well, from now on, she *will* like coffee.

'What time shall we meet?'

'Let's say five past one. Up to one is Thomas time – we do the Bond Street galleries on Saturdays.' The bus comes; Francis gives her a shy peck on the cheek.

'You've just missed him,' Francis says when she arrives in Old Compton Street at five past one as requested. Laura is not sure whether he is sorry or relieved.

'We went to see the John Tunnards at the Beaux Arts,' he tells her. Laura tries to look as if she knows what he is talking about. She asks him what he is reading and he holds up a battered Everyman edition of Marlowe's *Dr. Faustus*. 'It's coming on at the New Theatre, not often done. Want to go?' He puts the book down and gets her a coffee. Then they walk across to Better Books in Charing Cross Road. Francis picks up a volume of Henry Treece poems called *The Black Season* and buys it. 'New Apocalypse, great stuff!' He talks about Henry Treece as if he were Keats or Shelley. Laura admits that she has not read much contemporary poetry; her anthologies end with the First World War.

They amble along Charing Cross Road hand in hand. 'Now, I want to know everything about you!' Francis says. Laura loves the way his mouth turns down rather than up when he smiles. She tells him about her grandparents and her father, and the barest minimum about her mother. He stops in the middle of the road.

'My God, that's monstrous! One has only heard, read about it, hardly believed...' he squeezes her hand hard. 'I'd never, never have known you weren't born and bred British; you haven't the least trace of an accent!' Laura likes Francis better and better.

'You have your mother!' he goes on.

'Yes,' Laura says.

By the time they have got to Green Park, Francis is telling her that he is about to start printing a little magazine on an ancient printing press he has recently bought. 'It's going to be called *Reflections!* Tom's contributed a piece of luminous prose for the first number.' Then he asks if she would like to help with the setting up. Yes, she would love to help. Arm in arm, stars bright above them, they cross the park. Gently, Francis draws her to himself and kisses her.

She goes to see him in his basement flat in Highbury. The printing press takes up a large friendly space in the sitting room. 'Over a hundred years old,' Francis says with pride. He shows her how to hold the composing stick and gives her a poem to set up. She begins to find her way round the type font; the letters make a satisfying click as they fall into place. 'Taken to it like a duck to water,' Francis says presently. Laura barely looks up from what she is doing. He gets up to ink the platen; they pull a proof of the short poem she has just set up – there are quite a lot of literals. She extracts the wrong letters, puts them carefully back into their right compartments in the font, finds the correct ones. They pull another proof – only a couple of commas out of place now.

This is how Laura spends her Saturdays, growing into what begins to feel like her real self. When they have finished printing, Francis gives her coffee in a pint-sized mug and those squashed fly Garibaldi biscuits they had during air raids in the cellar at Mentmore. He talks about Marlowe's *Faustus* and about the magical novels of Charles Williams, of whom Laura has not heard. He lends her *The Place of the Lion,* which grips her while she is reading it, but leaves nothing much in its wake.

One Saturday, instead of making coffee when they have finished setting up and printing, Francis takes her into his bedroom, undresses her, spends time gazing at her while her heart beats wildly. Now... now... now... Laura loses her virginity.

'Stay the night? Francis asks.

'My mother...' Laura says, thinking *wouldn't care,* but she would like Francis to think that she has a mother who *does* care. She wonders if somehow Ruth will be able to tell she is no longer a virgin. He sees her to the station, looks and looks at her, says 'My girl', is reluctant to let go of her hand as his mauve silk scarf flaps in the wind. *Do I truly love him?* Laura asks herself on the way home. *Was it wonderful?*

Unusually, Ruth is in when she gets back to West Hampstead. 'Come, here, come here, I vant to show you somesing!' Her eyes are shining. *This is what she must have looked like when she was young, before I happened to her,* Laura thinks. Ruth pats the place next to her on the sofa. 'Sit viz me a minute, dahlink!' She waves an envelope with exotic stamps at Laura, pulls a typed letter on blue air mail paper out of it. 'It's from Bangkok – he's alive – he's coming on leave to see us!' Laura, the feel of Francis's skin still on hers, looks bewildered.

'But who?'

'Bernard, our cousin Bernard!'

Slowly it dawns on Laura who this letter, which excites her mother so, is from. Bernard is her grandpa's nephew, closest to her in age in the family, though his being seventeen when she was only eight put a vast distance between them. He was sent out to Bangkok apprenticed to Unilever. Laura remembers how at the farewell supper for him what the old people talked about was whether the boy should wear Bermuda shorts on the voyage out, preening themselves on the fact that they knew what such things were. Light-hearted talk to mask the fact that they might never see him again. She also remembers her outrage when Bernard took the last helping of green ice cream that she had her eye on.

So, someone in the family has survived. This cousin is going to show up in flesh and blood.

'He vill be here in two veeks,' Ruth says.

'He can't possibly stay here,' Laura says at once. What

will Bernard, last seen surrounded by Berlin opulence, think of the way they live? When he sees the fluted coffee cups with the black and yellow flowers in that packing case dresser? Even though it is now covered with sheets dyed pale brown.

'He is staying viz a colleague, don't vorry!'

Laura goes to bed elated. She has a real live cousin. And she has a lover.

Bernard arrives with an enormous bunch of white lilies, the kind of bunches that were the thing in Berlin. Laura sees the glow of affection on his face, on Ruth's face, sees the family likeness – they have the same shiny brown eyes, the same downward turning mouths. Laura has forgotten for the moment that she, too, has those. Bernard blushes a little when he turns to her and shakes her warmly by the hand. She hopes he will not say something like *You've turned into a proper young lady*. No, he is better than that: he says, 'I can hardly believe I'm talking to both of you!' He tells them that his mother was deported the day he had all the papers for her to join him in Bangkok. Ruth tells him about her parents; Laura tells him about her father. Bernard bends over, kisses them on both cheeks. Perhaps this is what it might feel like to have a brother?

Ruth has put a yellow and white damask cloth on the table with matching napkins. There is apple strudel on a glass stand. 'Almost like Berlin!' she says. Laura sees Bernard wince.

He calls in every day. Ruth looks years younger. When Laura has to have a tooth out with gas, Bernard picks her up from the dentist and takes her arm as they walk out into the rain. 'My God, this weather,' he says, hailing a taxi.

'I'd like to take you both out to the theatre before my leave's up,' he says, 'though I shall need a bit of guidance.' He looks at Laura.

'You take my daughter, dahlink,' Ruth says, blinking her eyes at Bernard, 'I von't come.'

'Just as you like.' He sounds quite pleased.

Laura suggests Shaw's *St. Joan*. 'I read the part of Dunois at school,' she tells him. 'And a friend of mine was St. Joan, she was brilliant!' Bernard looks at her blankly.

'And we'll find somewhere to eat afterwards,' he says.

'I only know coffee places and British Restaurants and Lyons Cornerhouses!'

'You can leave the restaurant to me. How about Saturday?'

'Can't manage Saturdays,' Laura says, without mentioning Francis. She will ask Francis what he thinks of Shaw; probably not enough magic about him. Quite soon they are going to see *Dr. Faustus* and probably the mysterious Tom is coming with them.

Bernard has got tickets. He brings more flowers when he picks her up – huge yellow chrysanthemums. He gives them Siamese silk stoles. Laura can see he would like her to put hers on; she has never worn anything so luxurious. Ruth has thrown hers over her shoulders and is prancing about the room with it.

Bernard wants to get a taxi again, but Laura won't let him. 'It's quicker on the underground.'

'You do this a lot?'

'Every day; it's just part of life!'

They have seats in the front row of the dress circle and, when the curtain goes up, Laura is immediately enthralled, though she can tell from the way Bernard is flicking the pages of his programme that he is not enjoying the play much. During the interval, while they are sipping gin and tonics, he asks her to explain one or two things. 'Don't get much time for reading!' Laura cannot imagine a life without time for reading.

He has booked a table in a French restaurant in Old Compton Street. When Laura tells him it is less than ten minutes walk from where they are, he is surprised how well she knows her way about. 'I go to a coffee bar the other end of Old Compton Street,' is as close as she gets to telling her cousin about Francis.

It begins to rain. 'We should have got a taxi!' Bernard says as they get to the door of the restaurant.

They walk in through a velvet curtain. A man with slicked back hair bends over Laura's hand and kisses it. Are her nails quite clean? Another man helps them off with their coats. Laura is glad she is wearing the Siamese silk stole. They are shown to their table: their chairs are pulled back; menus in leather covers are brought. When she looks at hers, Laura knows she is out of her depth.

'You choose,' she says to Bernard.

'Well, it's either boeuf bourguignon or coq au vin,'

'You choose,' she says again – she has never eaten either.

Bernard orders the beef. Then he disappears behind the wine list.

'Something red, don't you think? How about Nuits St. Georges?'

Laura is flattered that he thinks she knows what that might be like. She does not want to say *you choose* again, so she just nods. She would like to get the ordering over so they can discuss the play, but the wine waiter has arrived with the bottle. Bernard scrutinises the label; the waiter pulls the cork and pours a drop into Bernard's glass. Bernard sniffs it, swills it round in his mouth.

'This is corked! Bring another bottle!'

'Sir!' The waiter disappears.

Laura is ready to sink through the floor. Bernard tucks the

napkin under his chin and waits for the new bottle. This one passes the test; he does not thank the waiter, so Laura does. She no longer feels like talking about the play. Bernard does live in a different world! He asks about her job.

'It's not wonderful, I'm not allowed to do editorial work, only clerical, because of the unions.'

'Oh, unions!' Bernard says acidly.

'But I'm going to find somewhere they'll let me do a bit of writing.'

'Like your father,' Bernard says and puts his hand on hers. There are not many people now who would know that.

'My leave's almost up,' he says.

'But you like *your* job?'

'On the whole. Not always easy being a manager, but I'm up for promotion again – assistant director next, though they prefer...' He stops to wipe his mouth and does not finish the sentence.

'They prefer?' Laura asks.

'I was hoping...' Bernard's voice trails away again.

The waiter brings the bill; Bernard pulls a thick wad of notes out of his wallet and puts some in the leather folder.

It is still raining when they get outside, so this time Laura does not stop him from getting a taxi. 'I was hoping,' he begins again and puts his arm through hers as they settle back in the taxi, 'I was hoping to take a wife back with me. Is there any chance you would...' Again he leaves the sentence unfinished. He picks it up again with, 'It's not a bad life out there, better than...' Laura knows he was going to say *better than this awful place you live in now, better than going to some office on the underground every morning.* She does not blame him for thinking that, but blames him for not realising he has ruined that sense of familial affection so lacking in her life. She moves away from him in the taxi.

Back up in the flat, she sees Ruth look at him questioningly. Then her mother knew he was going to… Was that why she didn't come with them? Laura stands there forlorn while Ruth and Bernard chat.

'Ven vill ve see you again?' Ruth asks as he is leaving.

'Next year, with a bit of luck!'

Laura runs downstairs after him.

'You know, I do love you, you're my cousin, you're what's left of the family, that's how I love you!' She puts her arms round him and hugs him.

'I know. I'm sorry,' he says and leaves quickly. Laura can see he is very upset.

The days feel empty without him.

'You know, ven he vas a boy…' Ruth says.

'Yes? When he was a boy?'

'He vore green knickerbockers. Harris tveed, and ve said k-nickerbockers,' she adds, sounding the k. They laugh. Laura waits for Ruth to go on; she can sense her remembering things she is not saying.

'Such a nice boy! How happy you vould have been viz him!'

'I'm happy with my boyfriend Francis!'

Laura goes to her room.

§

She starts a letter to Hannah to tell her about this cousin who turned up out of the blue but does not mention that he wanted to take her back to Bangkok. She also tells Hannah about Francis and his printing press and that perhaps, later, he might allow her to contribute a piece. She has been keeping a notebook. And she has registered for evening classes in Latin so that she can go ahead to do an Arts degree. The letter flows freely; it is so much easier to say things to Hannah than to her mother. And yet, since Bernard's visit, things have been easier between them. They lead their separate lives; there does not seem to be a man in Ruth's life, though occasionally someone called Benny occurs in the conversation. Laura does not press for details; she has a man of her own now and has a feeling her mother respects her for that – much more than for any academic ambitions.

Making love with Francis grows in intensity. He cannot wait to take her clothes off, to gaze before touching. Laura is amazed at the response he kindles in her, the almost unbearable sweetness. So she is a little affronted when, fully dressed again and ready to begin printing, Francis looks at her balefully and asks, 'What happens to us?' almost as if he wishes nothing had happened.

'You know what happens,' Laura says sharply. Perhaps it is not really love?

One Saturday Laura arrives early at the Old Compton Street café. She sees Francis talking to a broad-faced young man who is gesticulating with large hands.

'Hallo, you're early!' Francis says and Laura feels reprimanded. 'Tom, this is Laura, Laura – Tom,' Francis looks anxiously from one to the other.

I will not say *I'm sorry to be early* Laura thinks as she hears herself say, 'I am sorry to be early!'

'Tom's just about to go.' Francis looks at his friend, who shows no sign of leaving.

'You're coming to the Marlowe with us?' Tom asks Laura. He has good grey eyes.

'Of course she is, next Friday!' Francis says.

Laura would have liked to reply herself. Tom gets up, swinging a shabby music case.

'His great thoughts in that', Francis says.

Tom smiles at Laura. He has jaggedy teeth.

They go to see *Dr. Faustus.* Robert Eddison is a magnificently malign Mephistopheles to Cedric Hardwicke's tortured Faustus.

'Tonight I'll conjure, though I die for it!' Tom whispers sepulchrally as they walk out of the theatre into the damp night. Francis stops stock still in the middle of Charing Cross Road and shouts *'Christ cannot save thy soul, there's none but I have interest in the same!'* His mauve silk scarf flies out behind him in the wind. People turn round and stare. 'Yes, Harry Andrews was awfully good as Lucifer, wasn't he?' Laura says to cover her embarrassment. The two boys on either side of her grab her arms. 'We'll walk home,' they say and cross into Tottenham Court Road. They live quite close to each other.

'But…' Laura begins, then stops. Here and now, between these two young Englishmen there are no *buts;* she is released from otherness, is fully alive in the present – *that* is the magic.

It begins to rain. Tom, not Francis, opens his umbrella and holds it over her. By the time they get to Warren Street, the magic is beginning to wear thin.

'I'll get myself home from here,' Laura says.

'You're coming home with me, my girl,' Francis tells her.

'Printing tomorrow,' Laura says and turns quickly into the station without looking at either of them.

On the escalator down she feels a new and intoxicating sense of freedom. She belongs to no one but herself.

It is past midnight by the time she gets back to West Hampstead, still feeling elated. The light is out in her mother's room but she hears murmured voices. It takes her a long time to fall asleep. Idiotically, she is thinking *Why wasn't it Francis who held an umbrella over me?* She seems still to be thinking that when she hears Ruth's voice. 'Vakee, vakee!' Laura opens her eyes to see her mother offering her a cup of tea.

'Drink zis, zen come and have breakfast viz us!'

'Us?'

When she opens the sitting room door, she sees there, facing her, a man with a drooping moustache, stark naked.

'Zis is Benny!'

'Come in, come in; don't be shy,' Benny says from under his moustache.

Why isn't *he* shy?

Back in her room, Laura makes a decision: she will move out. What kind of mother dishes up naked men for breakfast? This mother! Buoyed up by the new found sense of belonging only to herself, she tells Francis what she has decided without mentioning what triggered the decision.

'Great,' he says, 'find somewhere round here!' But he does not suggest she move in with him.

Tom arrives to help with the printing. 'Speed things up a bit,' he says and asks Laura if she got home all right.

Laura is not quite sure whether Francis is pleased – he begins to hum loudly. She makes more mistakes than usual with the setting up; she cannot get rid of the image of Benny's veined torso and her mother's sickly smile. They pull a proof, correct it and put the press to bed under its striped blanket. When Francis has given them coffee, he announces that he will be away for a conference the following weekend.

'Come to a concert with me?' Tom asks Laura.

'Yes, good idea, keep her out of mischief,' Francis says. He never goes to concerts, blithely admitting that he is tone deaf. Laura would like to make her own decisions.

'What's the concert?' she asks.

'Beethoven quartets. Rasoumovsky 59 Nos 1 and 2; the Loewenguth playing at the YM in Great Russell Street.' Tom's eyes are shining, but it conveys very little to Laura. She has only ever been to proms at the Albert Hall.

'I'm not sure,' she says, not because she would not like to hear Beethoven quartets but because... The reasons fizzle out unformulated. As Francis is seeing Tom out, she hears him ask 'How's that mature lady you've been seeing?'

'Oh her,' is all that Tom says.

'You know I love you, my dear,' Francis whispers as they are lying on his bed in the dark.

'I love you, too.' But even as she is saying it, Laura is not absolutely sure. How can you ever be absolutely sure? It is so long since she felt absolutely sure anyone loved her – like her granny and grandpa, like her father.

On the day, Laura decides there is no reason why she should not go to the chamber concert. She has not seen Tom again and on the way it occurs to her that she might not be able to get a ticket. Well, if not, not – *che sera sera*, that line from the Marlowe has stuck.

She does get a ticket, looks round for Tom but does not see him. The lights dim; the musicians settle down round a standard lamp. As they begin to play, Laura is taken out of herself into a dimension where thought is replaced by a sense of wholeness which stays with her even when the music has stopped and the Loewenguth quartet are bowing to rapturous applause. The lights go up. She feels a ping on her head, puts her hand up to find a pellet of paper. *Look up*, it tells her. She does and there is Tom waving from the balcony.

'See you later,' he mouths at her.

The quartet begin to play again. No music has ever stirred Laura like this. There is a moment of rapt silence between the last note and the applause, which goes on and on. At last, people move slowly towards the exit. Laura moves with them. Tom is standing outside, his dark hair tousled in the wind.

Please don't say anything, Laura prays. He says nothing, takes her hand in his large paddy one; they walk along in silence.

'Let's eat,' Tom says when they get to Shearn's vegetarian restaurant in Tottenham Court Road. Laura has been there once or twice with Francis: they don't go often – it is too expensive. When they are sitting down inside, the only reference Tom makes to the concert is 'I thought you'd come!'

On a mild March Saturday morning she finds a room less than ten minutes walk from where Francis lives, not much further from Tom, though she has not visited him. The landlady in her flowery pinny, who is not over-friendly, takes Laura up two flights of stairs into a fair-sized room with a sash window overlooking tree tops. The furniture is adequate: there is a small sink in one corner and a gas ring. The landlady pulls a flap from the top of the gas fire.

'Another ring 'ere, and I'll replace these,' she points to three broken elements in the gas fire. 'And 'ere's the meter; takes bobs and tanners; bathroom one floor down. Rent's 17/6d a week, payable in advance. And no gentlemen callers after nine pm!'

Laura can afford that: she earns £4 5/- a week now, working for a small publisher in Soho who syndicates magazines for factory workers. She is writing all the pieces except the sports page. The American editor Hank sees to that and sometimes he edits what Laura has written, cutting words like *quotidian* and *nevertheless* which, according to him, would put factory workers off. Apart from him, there is only the director Mrs. L, which is all she ever calls herself; she has a head of shiny red curls and green fingernails. Neither she nor Hank blinked an eyelid when Laura said her German name, Mrs. L even spelt it correctly. Of course, Laura knows that what she writes at work is hardly *writing* compared with what goes into the little magazine she has been helping to produce. She arranges to move in the following Saturday, pays and leaves her name. The landlady looks her up and down, says,

'That's never an English name!'

'No,' Laura says and walks away.

The raffia chimney sweep and the little goldfinch glass cage are on the windowsill; a pink and white damask tablecloth that Ruth has given her is spread on the table. With the bit of herself that still thinks the label *mother* ought to mean what the word leads one to expect, Laura wishes Ruth had come to see her into her new room. But then, if Ruth were that kind of mother, she would not be in this room. Laura is annoyed with herself when she feels tears rising. She will *not* cry: she is exactly where she wants to be.

She puts her hand on a blue envelope which is lying on the pink tablecloth. It is a letter from Hannah; the crinkly white £5 note that came with it is in her wallet. Laura makes a cup of tea with an egg-shaped metal tea infuser that leaks leaves into the cup; perhaps she will spend Hannah's fiver on a teapot. She reads the letter again. Hannah has invited her to spend a weekend in Yorkshire; Klaus has been made consultant anaesthetist at the local hospital.

I'll go, Laura thinks, *it'll give me a breathing space.* What does she need a breathing space for? She has just moved into a room of her own, is enjoying her job, so… What she needs the breathing space for is to ask herself whether she is getting too fond of Tom. He has asked her to another concert; she has said no, not because she did not want to accept but because she is Francis's girlfriend. The three of them have spent several evenings stapling red card covers on two hundred copies of *Reflections* and trimmed them with Francis's guillotine. To celebrate they went to see *Le Jour se lève* with Jean Gabin at the

Hampstead Everyman Cinema. Laura felt just as comfortable with Tom's arm against hers as with Francis's. She loves the tweed jacket with its flecks of many colours that Tom wears; she wishes Francis would not always, always wind that mauve silk scarf round his neck. But if you love someone, then what they wear is not important, is it? Besides, the times she has with Francis when neither of them is wearing anything are wonderful. Are they? Aren't they? What would such times be like with Tom? If she finds out, will she become like her mother – this man today, another tomorrow?

Ruth still has not been to see her, but she rings on Saturday mornings. Laura hates it when the landlady yells up 'That foreign lady on the phone for you again!' Ruth tells her she is thinking of going to Berlin to visit old friends who have survived the war. 'Half Jewish, like you,' her mother says and Laura somehow feels disowned by that remark. 'I go ven ze Russian blockade is over. I sink ze Americans are vonderful viz this airlift, don't you?' Laura has been too taken up with her own life to take much notice of the news – what's happening in Berlin no longer has anything to do with her now that her father and her grandparents are dead. 'You heppy in your own room, my big daughter?' Ruth changes the subject. 'Yes, thank you, you'll have to come and see it, won't you!'

Laura puts the receiver down.

She goes to Yorkshire. Hannah and Klaus live in a Victorian grey stone house at the top of a steep drive. Laura gives Hannah a blue and white vase she saw in Heals; she spent that fiver on it, remembering how her granny told her always to give presents you would like to keep yourself. 'For me?' Hannah gives Laura a hug. They have tea, not coffee, for breakfast. 'You see? we've become quite English,' Klaus says, helping himself to porridge. 'By the way, has my wife told you her news?' Laura is moved by the way he says *my wife* with such pride. It must make you feel safe to be called that.

'I passed my driving test, second try,' Hannah says.

'Not that, dearie, your work!'

'Oh yes, I'm teaching German at the Grammar School here – only part-time,' she adds modestly. Klaus gets up, pats Laura on the head, pecks Hannah on the cheek and takes himself off to his hospital.

'Shall we go to the Brontë Parsonage in Haworth, it's quite near?' Hannah asks.

On the drive there, Laura wishes Hannah would stop talking about *Jane Eyre* and poor Mr. Rochester because she has almost driven through red lights and keeps stalling up hills. 'I need more practice,' Hannah admits when they get to Haworth.

No wonder the Brontës wrote what they did, Laura thinks, looking at the heavy moss-covered tombstones in the churchyard. When they have finished walking round the house, Hannah buys a copy of *Jane Eyre* with the parsonage stamp in it for Laura. As she is paying, the woman at the till says 'It's so nice to have visitors from abroad coming again! Where are you from?' Rather peeved, Hannah says, 'Actually, I'm quite local – I live just outside Keighley!' The woman gives her the change without further comment.

Driving back, Hannah says, 'I don't intend to retail my life story every time I go into a shop! Though I don't suppose we'll ever count as really English, British passport or not!'

I will, Laura thinks stubbornly. She is determined not to wear the refugee label for the rest of her life.

Later, relaxing in front of the sitting room fire, Klaus uncorks a bottle of Burgundy.

'Got a case of this from someone whose stomach we repaired!' They clink glasses.

'Lechayim, here's to Eretz Israel!'

Israel declared independence a few months earlier, though that news did not touch Laura any more than the advent of the Berlin airlift. The arrival of West Indians on the *Windrush* has made a greater impression; she feels for them when she sees notices in the windows of bed-and-breakfast places saying *No Blacks*. They remind her of the *Juden Unerwünscht* signs plastered all over Berlin.

'I can't wait to go and see my cousin who's settled in Tel Aviv,' Hannah says.

'As soon as I can get away, dearie!'

'You wouldn't go and live there?' Laura asks anxiously.

'Well, you never know...' Hannah says.

'We belong here now!' Klaus says, to Laura's great relief.

She opens up and tells them about her job, writing those pieces about films and beauty products and London parks; about the little magazine she has been helping to print, about Francis and Tom and how she loves going about with them.

'And who do you like best?' Hannah asks.

'Oh Francis, of course!'

But she talks about Tom.

'He's getting himself as second degree, in philosophy – it's what he's always wanted to do. Didn't do well in zoology because he hated dissecting those rabbits and things; he's just teaching at a crammers for the moment.'

'And what does your Francis do?'

Laura is a touch uncomfortable with that *your.*

'He works in a lab doing experiments with chlorophyll or something – and he writes poems!'

She tells them about going to do Latin in evening classes so she can go on to do an English degree.

'Could you manage all that with a full time job?'

'Yes!'

'How old are you now?'

'Nineteen!'

'The whole of life before you, lucky girl! And as for boy-friends, don't rush into anything, there's plenty of time!'

'Only I don't want to…' she does not finish the sentence, she was going to say *become like my mother.*

Not long after Laura has got back from Yorkshire, Ruth finally comes to see her in Highbury.

'I vant to tell you somesing, my independent daughter,' and she leans forward to stroke Laura's cheek.

'Yes?'

'Vell, now you've made a life for yourself, I have decided to move to America!'

'Really?' Laura asks in a daze.

'You remember Henry?'

Laura wishes she did not.

'Vell, he alvays promised to get me over to Chicago.'

'But…' Laura knows Henry has long been with another woman.

'Ve're still good friends,' Ruth adds quickly.

'And Benny?'

Ruth looks at the floor. 'I have to admit, zat vas a mistake!'

'I thought you were thinking of going to Berlin?'

'Yes, I vanted to go, but zis is more important – a new life for me!'

Ruth pulls out a bundle from her carrier bag. Wrapped in a red-bordered drying up cloth are the silver-plated fish knives and forks from Berlin.

'I sought you vould like zese!'

What is Laura going to do with a dozen fish knives and forks?

'Ze ozzer sings I take viz me,' Ruth tells her.

'You think you'll like Chicago enough to live there?'

'Vy not?'

Laura does not go to see her mother off, because on that day she has an interview at Birkbeck College. It goes well. Provided she gets her Latin Intermediate, she will be welcome in the English department. Good. She goes back home, yes *home,* to Highbury. She has the day off work. Mrs. L and Hank are encouraging about her proposed degree course; besides, they are winding up the business – not enough factories have opted for those syndicated magazines. They have told Laura to find a new job and will go on paying her until she has. Hank tells her to dip her hand into the petty cash on Fridays. 'No one's looking!' How different from that trade union house in Long Acre! Better or worse? Mrs. L and Hank have given her the chance to try her hand at a bit of journalism; the other job offered security, but for the moment Laura can afford to flout security.

She fingers a letter in her pocket which arrived in the morning post. It is from Tom. There is a photograph of him and a note telling her he has fallen in love with her. When can they meet? Something inside Laura falls into place. Yes, she will see Tom; she will not let Francis make love to her again. But she has to see Francis that very evening: his mother has come up from the country specially to meet her; they are going to Christopher Fry's *Ring Round the Moon.*

'What a tremendous help you've been with the magazine,' Francis's mother says. She has pink country cheeks and grey eyes that radiate good will.

'Oh yes, and Tom as well,' Laura says, feeling terrible.

'Nice boy.' But there is something iffy about the way Francis's mother says that.

'You must come and stay with us,' she goes on, 'Francis will show you his favourite walks through our woods!'

No, she will not do that.

Laura cannot wait for the play to begin, but when it does she cannot concentrate. How to begin to tell Francis that... that... He takes her hand; she lets it lie inert in his.

She has sleepless nights, answers one or two advertisements for jobs, but not Tom's letter. There is a picture postcard of Chicago from Ruth. On Saturday she does not go to see Francis as usual though he is expecting her. Quite late in the evening, he calls round.

'Is all well, my dear?' he asks, and Laura can tell he knows that it is not.

'I thought your mother was still with you,' Laura lies. She hates doing that.

Francis gives her a copy of Hermann Hesse's *Siddhartha,* which has just come out in English. She could, of course, have read it in German. She backs away when he tries to kiss her, then stretches out her hand when she sees the pain in his eyes. Perhaps she does still love him?

'I'm going to have to concentrate on my Latin,' she says. 'You have Tom to help you with the printing.'

'I see.' Francis's whole body sags; his head droops. 'Then I'll leave you to your Latin,' he says so softly she can barely hear it. She has not yet written to Tom.

She gets one of the jobs she applied for, a bit of a dogsbody appointment with a publisher in Piccadilly, where she will be working for two people. The first is an ex-RAF pilot with a grey handlebar moustache who tells her he does not know the first thing about publishing and will expect to learn a great deal from her.

'For instance, what the hell do they mean by format, do you think?' he asks, looking at some papers on his desk.

'Shape and size of things?' Laura says diffidently.

'Good old girl!' He gets up and shakes Laura's hand.

The second person is a rather fierce-looking not-quite-young woman who says she wants to put Shakespeare on the map. She peers at Laura. 'I was really hoping for a blonde ferret, but I suppose you'll do!'

Laura is introduced to the director, who tells her he himself might occasionally call on her. 'When there's a crisis,' he says, laughing. Laura says *Yes* to everything. The salary is £4 10/- a week – five bob more than she has been earning. No one has asked about the provenance of her surname.

Pleased with herself, Laura takes the short cut through Swallow Street across Regent Street into Brewer Street, where she buys herself a quarter of humbugs to celebrate; sweets have come off points, though everything else is still rationed. Back in the office, Mrs. L and Hank wish her luck and give her a month's holiday pay. Hank tells her that two guys have been on the phone wanting to talk to her, urgently.

She does not return the phone calls and takes a week's break between jobs. She wanders up and down Charing Cross Road, in and out of the Old Compton Street café. She spends time looking at what is on the round table in Better Books: Kafka's *The Trial* has just come out in English – Francis has talked about that. There is Orwell's *Animal Farm* and Aldous Huxley's *Brave New World* – Tom has mentioned those. How she misses them on either side of her, talking to and across her. She buys all three books with some of her holiday pay. On her way out, she sees copies of *Reflections* on the rack with the other magazines: *Horizon, Partisan Review, Outposts, Twentieth Century*. She buys a copy of *Reflections*, although she has three copies of it at home, and re-reads Francis's introduction with its insistence on the importance of fantasy, fable and journals and Tom's piece of prose poetry, which is like an abstract painting of an autumn morning. She tries, and fails, to read these pieces as if she did not know the people who wrote them. The only shadowy way that she exists in the magazine is an acknowledgment of help from friends with the printing.

She takes herself back into the café with her new books. There is iron foot Jack; there is the young man who wears purple silk socks and carries a twee little shopping basket; there is the bag lady, her skirt held up by a large safety pin, fluting away in her Chelsea voice, *My deah, I was the belle of Paris...* No Francis; no Tom. Back at home in Highbury, there is post: a note from Francis, claiming he cannot live without her. Tom, writing from Yorkshire where he is taking a break with his mother, claims that he cannot live without her. *And without whom can't I live?* Laura asks herself, without allowing an answer to surface. She begins a letter to Francis. She will not be able to get out of hurting him. *He'll get over it*, she tells herself; *I mustn't overestimate my own importance.* She scrumples the letter up and begins a letter to Tom. Yes, she looks forward to meeting him... flings the sheet of paper across the room; makes a cup of tea, swallows it too hot.

There are three more letters: a printed notice informing Old Mentmore Girls that, following the death of the elder Miss Thomas, the school is to close. Miss Elizabeth has scribbled a note saying she is staying on in the middle house in the Crescent and would be very pleased to see Laura, if ever she felt inclined to visit. Laura feels much more inclined still to be sitting in one of Miss Elizabeth's English classes.

There is a letter from Hannah, who writes as affectionately as ever – soon Laura must come again; they are about to adopt a nine year old boy, having given up hope of having children of their own, and are getting a puppy for him. Laura wishes she were nine years old again and someone would buy her a puppy; but when she was nine... She picks up the raffia chimney sweep.

There is a bulky envelope from America, the writing on it in bright blue ink unchanged since those Saturday morning letters at school on which she relied to make her feel like the others; now a pair of nylons falls out of the envelope. Ruth writes that things are not going well: she has had a gallstone attack; Henry's woman is a bitch; as soon as she has scraped the fare together, she will be back in London. The letter veers off into maudlin endearments. There is a PS saying that if the worst comes to the worst, if she cannot find the money, it might be necessary to leave the china, glass, linen, silver behind in exchange for the fare back to London. *Those things are mine as well,* Laura thinks with some bitterness. Then she remembers the fuss her grandpa used to make when the maid broke a Meissen china cup or, God help her, a Dresden figurine – she got the sack immediately. In the end, her granny had to pretend it was *she* who had broken whatever it was. Laura stops caring about the things her mother might leave behind in Chicago.

She decides it is not good enough to write to Francis. She must go to see him. She will tell him how much their times together have meant to her. Now.

'I knew you'd come, I knew…' he says when he sees her. No, he does not know. Laura gets him to come out for a walk; she will not go inside.

'I think Tom and I…' she begins.

'Have you slept with him?'

'No!'

'I don't believe you!'

This is not how it was meant to go. He has not given her chance to say what she intended. So instead she says,

'I can't help that!'

He grabs her by the shoulders.

'And you and me? Has all that meant nothing?'

The mauve scarf blows against his face, muffling his words. Laura pulls away from him.

'Of course it has meant something, meant a great deal but...' But, looking at his face distorted with anger, she cannot bring herself to go on.

'He's incapable of love, you'll find out!' he yells.

Laura turns away from Francis. His words penetrate her back like shrapnel. *Dear God,* she prays when she is back in her room, *show me... show me...* Laura does not know how to put into words what she needs to be shown. It is a long time since she has said or thought any kind of prayer, in English, German or Hebrew. She remembers wanting to go to church when she was at school, not because she believed in God or Jesus but because she wanted to be like the others; she remembers how, after the air raid on Weston when Molly called her a Jerry, she murmured the *Shma Yisroel* her granny had taught her. She did believe in God then, but now she is not at all sure if there is anyone to pray to – God is just another word, isn't it? But even as she thinks this, she knows it is not quite true, that perhaps God and Truth mean the same thing and that she is far from knowing *what* that is, only that, in some mysterious way, it *is*.

The moment she sees Tom standing on her doorstep, Laura feels a great burden drop from her.

Inside, they sit opposite each other, breathless with love. She strokes the lapel of his many coloured coat. 'Well!' he says and again 'Well!' and 'Here we are then!'

And. They are making love. Laura does not know where her body ends and his begins; it does not matter who is who in this ecstasy of oneness.

They fall into tranquil sleep. In the morning, Tom sings

'La Donna e mobile' joyfully in the bathroom.

'Miss Laura, Miss Laura,' the landlady screeches, 'I want ter see yer, come down ere this minnit!'

Laura puts her hand over her mouth. She had forgotten all about the embargo on gentlemen callers.

'Is that a man I can 'ear singing in the bathroom?'

'That's funny,' Laura says. 'I thought I heard it too!'

The landlady tilts her head to one side. 'Thank Gawd for that then. There's nothing wrong with me 'earing!'

Laura runs back up two steps at a time. Tom can't stop laughing when she tells him. 'Good sport, your landlady! We'll have to find somewhere to live together, won't we!' *Together!* Lovely word! Tom goes on, 'I went to see Francis before I came to you. He's taking it badly; says the bottom's fallen out of his life, doesn't know if the ground's going to be there when he puts his foot down, and it's all my fault. Shame it had to happen like this. We've been friends since our first year in college. Well, eventually he'll get over it!'

Laura does not tell Tom what Francis said about him.

They have breakfast; coffee has never smelt so good. 'What a great tablecloth!' Tom says, passing his hand over the pink and white patterns on it. Laura explains its provenance and goes on to talk about her mother in Chicago, about her grandparents and her father and how they died. Tom reaches across the table and holds her hand.

'Just goes to prove, if it still needed proving, what fools people are who believe in any kind of God!'

Laura is startled into drinking her coffee too hot.

After quite a long silence, she says, 'I'm not sure... You don't think perhaps, in a way...'

'Certainly not!' Tom interrupts her before she can finish the sentence. 'I knew it was all mumbo jumbo by the time I was fourteen, told the priests at school as much...'

'You went to a Catholic school?'

Tom nods. 'They told me to shut up and get on with my work, which I did. The biology master was a layman; he became my friend, helped me get into college.'

'What about your parents?'

'My Irish dad had to promise to bring up any children Catholic when he married Mam. She didn't care one way or the other, but she wasn't too pleased when Father This and Father That kept calling round after Dad died to see she was doing things right.'

'But how can you be quite so certain there isn't a God?'

'Easy – I'm a naïve realist!'

Laura is not quite sure what that means, but when she looks at Tom she *is* quite sure she loves him. And it occurs to her that God *does* have something to do with that.

They finish their breakfast. 'Come to see where I live?' Tom asks. On the wall of his quite small book-lined room, there is a photograph of a very beautiful woman.

'My grandmother,' Tom says, grinning.

'Really?'

'Don't be daft, that's Virginia Woolf!'

Laura goes red with embarrassment. They read *A Room of One's Own* at school, but she has not read any of the novels.

'Committed suicide a few years ago, kept on going mad,' Tom speaks dryly. He pulls a volume off the shelf. '*The Waves* – marvellous. No one else can do what she does!'

He opens the book and begins to read aloud. The luminous prose flows between them.

§

Ruth has come back to London from Chicago; Tom and Laura go to see her. She has moved to a different street in

West Hampstead. On the way to see her, Laura can't help feeling a small frisson of elation triggered by the phrase *going to see my mother who has come back from America.* Beneath the elation, there is apprehension: what will Tom think of Ruth?

'Laura's so pleased to have you back!' Tom says to her when they arrive.

His saying that helps Laura to make it so. She looks round the room.

'You look for our sings? I had to leave everysing in Chicago, vouldn't have got back ozzervise! And I vouldn't have got zis room if Bernard hadn't sent me somesing! But now I manage, still have friends here! Not Benny, don't vorry!'

Good of Bernard to help Ruth. Laura thinks of him with affection and hopes he finds a wife; then they could perhaps go on being cousins.

Ruth gives Laura two pairs of nylons.

'Quite a character your mother, isn't she!' Tom says later.

Laura is relieved that is how Tom puts it. 'Her accent's ghastly, isn't it!'

'Just wait til you meet mine! *Eee, our Laura, cum raht in, you must be starved.* She has her own accent, has me Mam!'

All that is left to show Tom is a Northerner are his short a's.

They think about finding somewhere to live together, somewhere in a different part of London where they will not run into Francis. Tom suggests putting an ad in *The New Statesman.* 'How about *Young married couple seeks...*'

'No, no!' Laura interrupts him. 'Young *un*married couple...' She will not pretend to be his wife before she is. When she thinks about marriage, she sees her granny and grandpa at the large dining table in Berlin. Her granny passes the most delicious morsel on her plate to him; he passes it back.

Whatever it is goes back and forth from plate to plate until it is not delicious any longer. Then they smile at each other in complete accord.

Tom and Laura are inundated with replies to their advertisement and settle on a large room in Kilburn with windows overlooking a long narrow garden with lime trees. They have their own bathroom! Bliss! When they move in, there is a jug of asters on their table; the couple who own the house give them a cup of tea and chocolate biscuits, and then they are left agreeably to themselves.

Tom has found a job teaching at a boys' grammar school. 'The headmaster asked if I was married. I said *almost!*'

Laura tries her hand at cooking; she buys rock salmon so they can use the fish knives. Tom just pushes it about on his plate. He doesn't notice the fish knives and forks with the sea creatures embossed on them.

'You know rock salmon's dogfish, don't you? he says. 'And I've been dissecting it all day with the boys!'

No, she did not know.

He leans across the table and kisses her.

'I'm not marrying you for your culinary skills!'

'For my brains, of course!'

They laugh and laugh.

They go to spend Christmas with Tom's Mam in Middlesbrough. Ruth has gone to Berlin.

Laura leans against the antimacassar on the head rest of the plush Pullman train seat. The pink light of the little cornucopia lamp shines on *The New Statesman,* which she is not reading. The table is laid for lunch. Tom orders sherries.

'You won't be getting sherry at my Mam's,' he tells her; 'more like iron brew or dandelion and burdock!'

Laura watches the waiters as they balance heavy metal

trays on the palm of one hand, undulating with the movement of the train. Not a drop of anything gets spilt.

A coalman's cart is standing outside the small terrace house when they arrive; the horse has its head inside the front window – Tom's Mam is feeding it apples. The moment she sees Tom and Laura, she opens the front door and the horse takes its head out of the front room.

'Cum raht in, ee, you must be starved!'

They step inside. Tom got the sound of her exactly right. There, on a gate-leg table, is a bottle of sherry. Tom looks startled when he sees it; Laura grins at him. Tom's Mam follows their glances. 'Oh aye, Uncle Alfred brought that yesterday; thought you'd cum; wants us to go round there Boxing Day.' Tom's eyes turn bright turquoise as he looks at his mother, but they don't touch. Laura sees she has the same broad paddy hands as her son.

Tom carries their things upstairs into a backroom with a window overlooking a coal shed and outside lavatory in the backyard.

'Dad used to lock me in there when I'd done something wrong,' he says.

'Like what?' Laura asks appalled.

'Don't remember!'

But Laura can see he does.

Tom's Mam comes in. 'Tek her things next door, ee, our Laura, you won't mahnd sharing mah bed, will you?'

Share a bed with a total stranger? 'Doesn't she know we're living together?' she asks Tom while his Mam is busy in the back kitchen.

'Of course, but what would the neighbours think if we slept in the same room, not married?'

'How would they know?'

'How wouldn't they!'

The doubled bed Laura is sharing with Tom's Mam is wide enough for them not to have to touch. Laura tries not to take more than her fair share of the blankets. The thin paisley eiderdown slips to the bottom of the bed.

They have roast beef and Yorkshire pudding for Christmas dinner. Tom's Mam brings in steaming platefuls for them but, not sitting down, disappears into the back kitchen. Laura gets up to ask her to sit with them. 'Ah'll have mahn after, our Laura!' But Laura insists, and at last the three of them are sitting at the table together.

Tom has put out shiny red crackers. 'Never saw these for the duration, did we!' They join hands to pull them and put on their paper crowns. Tom's Mam tells Laura about the time he was so hungry when he came home from school that he put furniture polish on his bread instead of dripping. 'Raht gormless, our Tom, always has bin,' she says, beaming at him.

On Boxing Day, Uncle Alfred comes to pick them up in his Austin 7. He is a baker and has made a fortune during the war with some synthetic cream he dreamt up that tasted almost like the real thing. His wife, Auntie Pearl, Tom's Mam's prettier sister, never helped in the shop, too ladylike for that – too ladylike, as well, to have children.

When they arrive at the bungalow, Auntie Pearl offers Laura a limp hand to shake. 'Very pleased to meet you, Ah'm sure,' she says; Laura is not convinced. Tom's Mam sits uneasily on an armchair with petit point roses embroidered on it. They have tea in ivy-bordered bone china cups. There are small squares of Christmas cake arranged in a pyramid on a green leaf plate. Laura admires that. 'Ee, Ah've got one just lahk it, never use it; you're welcome to it, luv, if you fancy it!' Tom's Mam says.

Uncle Alfred looks at them with a conspiratorial smile. 'How was your cake then?' he asks.

'Delicious,' Laura says. It was.

'Last year's, weren't it!' Uncle Alfred is triumphant.

The next day they go to see Tom's school friend Alex, who lives in a leafy suburb. His father is a retired headmaster who tested and passed Tom for his eleven plus. There is a large family party going on in their house, in which the furniture has seen better days and the carpets are faded. Alex's mother, in a high-necked white blouse, reminds Laura of the great aunts who used to gather at her granny's coffee parties.

'I hear you're from Germany,' Alex's father says to her. 'Well, the war's over, thank God!' *As if I were an enemy he's forgiven?* Laura wonders.

When they play charades and she is swathed in a heavy green and gold brocade curtain from the dressing-up box, Laura, as Queen Boadicea, stops agonising about what people might or might not be thinking about her – she is enjoying herself in this lively family gathering. But when the charades are over and they are sipping mulled wine, Laura hears someone on the other side of the room say 'Jewish? I don't believe it! Ghastly bunch of money grubbers, Jews! I don't blame Hitler for persecuting them! But she seems such a nice girl!' Oddly enough, that remark does not disturb Laura too much. She feels safe with Tom about; there will always be prejudiced people – she does not have to know them, nor they her.

Alex sees her and Tom to the bus stop. 'I could wring my cousin's neck. What a moronic remark! I'm really sorry!' He pats Laura on the shoulder. 'Oh, it doesn't matter,' she says and means it. The bus comes. Alex waves, 'Invite me to the wedding, won't you,' he shouts.

They say goodbye to Tom's Mam. She has wrapped up her green leaf plate and gives it to Laura.

'You'll come and see us in London, Mam,' Tom says, his eyes lighting up again.

'Ah will an' all, and mebbe Ah'll get to meet your Mam, our Laura?'

'But where will she stay?' Laura asks Tom on the way back to Kings Cross, not in a Pullman train this time.

'We'll find a b & b near us.'

'Whatever will our mothers talk about if they meet?' Laura can't imagine. Or perhaps she is imagining it too vividly?

'About us, I expect! By the way, Mam said that you've got an old head on young shoulders!'

'Is that good?'

For a moment Tom does not answer, then he says quietly, 'Everything about you is good!'

All doubt falls from Laura. She is as sure of Tom's love for her as she was of her grandparents' and her father's. She knows that without them behind her she could not have come through. She does not dwell too graphically on their terrible deaths: if time is circular, and perhaps it is, then their moments of full life are equally valid. She remembers her father pulling her on her sledge along Unter den Linden to the Christmas market in Berlin. She remembers her grandpa letting her peer down his microscope and her granny counting the linen, putting aside sheets and towels for when her little goldfinch gets married.

Happy together, Laura and Tom are asleep in their double bed. When they wake up, it will be their wedding day.

They wake up. Laura gets into her new blue dress with the row of tiny buttons all down the front and a wasp waist. She does not have a wasp waist, but this dress pretends she does. She makes sure the hat with the blue feather sits at exactly the right angle on her head. Tom is wearing his father's three piece suit; she has never seen him in a waistcoat, it makes him look so... so... so like a man about to be married? Side by side, they stand in front of the mirror.

'I can't believe it's really happening!' Laura says.

'Believing doesn't come into it, it just *is!*' Tom tells her. He takes her hand in his.

§ § §